ASK GRACE

by

S.E. REED

For my husband and children—my loves, my inspiration.

Chapter One

Don't Ask Grace

My hands are resting on top of my head, covering my naturally copper-colored hair. After a few long seconds, I let them fall down to my sides, my shoulders slumping forward. I want to smash my face against the table instead of answering stupid questions.

"What was the question again?"

"What can you tell me about Gloria?" the detective asks.

This whole thing is so infuriating. I don't even know why they are asking me about her. As if I might know something big or important about what happened. "She's lived next-door to me my whole life." I state the most obvious fact about my neighbor, *Dollface*.

Write.

Scratch.

"And?"

"And what? She isn't one of my *real friends* or anything. You know, we hang out with different people." I take a deep breath and exhale loudly. This isn't rocket science here; I don't know why she's having such a hard time understanding me.

"And?" she asks again.

"And what! She's—she's—how do I put this delicately, Gloria is—" I pause. "Look, we don't talk!" I'm getting pissed off. I glance around the room and take in my surroundings. Mom and Dad are whispering in the arched doorway to the kitchen and they keep looking over at me with worried faces. That weird vein in Dad's thick neck is sticking out and pulsating—the one he says makes him look like a tough guy when he works out at the gym. But right now he just looks scared and I hate it.

Then there's my mom, with her stupid flowery apron, like she's fooling anyone. She doesn't cook, she just heats up meals from Costco or bakes that pre-made cookie dough and pretends it's homemade. That grimace says she's about to throw up, right into the pocket of her floral apron. She's probably had at least one ~~glass~~ bottle of Chardonnay. I can smell it, lingering in the air—tangy and pewtered. Why do adults think drinking wine is like a badge of honor?

I wish my parents would both just calm the eff down.

I'm having a hard enough time concentrating as it is without all their little whispery and secretive nonsense. It's like the Spanish Inquisition over here at the dining room table and sweat is dripping down my pale face. I know this entire experience is going to make me break out.

I use the side of my hand to push the hair and sweat out of my eyes. I wish my bangs would grow out already so I could tuck them behind my ears. Why did I cut bangs again? Oh yeah, because I'm an idiot and thought I'd look good. That's funny, because no one looks good in bangs, that is unless you followed that YouTube video, the one with the twist-over-swoop-snip. But seriously, who can cut their own hair like that?

Not me.

A radio crackles, and one of the two police officers, in their blue uniforms and bulletproof vests with handcuffs and guns strapped to them, reaches up and clicks the radio. He says something inaudible into it, and it stops making noise. They haven't moved in what feels like hours, just lingering by the mantle of our fake fireplace. It's definitely not helping this situation.

My nerves are shot!

Cops.

A detective.

Mom and Dad.

Oh crap. And right on cue a pins-and-needles sensation starts in my feet. It won't be long before it works its way up my spine. Once it hits my head, I'm done for. The radio crackles again.

"Roger that," the officer says. What are they doing just standing there? Shouldn't they be on the streets looking for the real criminals? Isn't that a thing—you know, the first forty-eight hours, it's like the only time to solve a crime. After that it's a cold case or something. I mean, am I the criminal here? Why are they even in my house?

Scratch, write, flip page.

I haven't said enough for her to do that much writing.

This entire thing is ridiculous.

I put my hand up to my temple and try to will the pain in my spine from rising any further. Then I check my watch. It's already nine-thirty.

Damn. I'm late. I was supposed to be at Nico's house an hour ago to record the next episode of our podcast: *What's in the Woods?* We started it is as a spoof with our other bestie Emma. It's like a fake *Stranger Things*... but about the monsters that live in the Loblolly Pine woods that surround Richmond Hill. At this rate, we're gonna have to postpone it until tomorrow night. I can already hear our twelve fans bitching in the comments. And then I'm going to have to get salty in my replies and remind them there AREN'T REAL MONSTERS in the woods and everything we say is just made-up crap for fun and not an actual investigation into the paranormal. Okay, so maybe the headless ghost from our first episode might be real, but that's the only one. Everything else is stupid.

The woman sitting across from me is tight-lipped. Her white-blonde hair is pulled into a severe bun and her face wrinkle-free, not in a good way from years of great skin care, but more like from having a stick up her ass and never laughing or smiling.

"Do you know if Gloria has any *other* close friends? Anyone we can talk to, who might have actual information?" She glares at me.

"What?" I blink and rub my eyes.

"I said, who can we talk to? Who knows Gloria?" It's clearly a struggle for her to keep her voice from getting shrill. She scribbles more in her teensy notepad when I don't instantly respond. Like, how many words can she actually fit on that micro-pad? She doesn't even have a front pocket to put it in like they do on cop shows. She's no Olivia Benson.

God, why do I keep thinking about cop shows? *The First-48. Law and Order.* I literally hate them! Week after week of pathetic, sad, fake tragedies ripped from the headlines. Why on earth do people watch those? Now take a full season of a Netflix horror or drama, with teens trying to solve a supernatural mystery—that's where my heart lies.

But ugh, if this thing around our dining room table keeps going the way it's going, with the cops and the questions, my life is going to be the headline of our local newspaper in the morning: *Teen questioned by cops all night until her head exploded, blood and guts splattering across the room like a Jackson Pollock.*

I'm not sure I can handle the pressure, not to mention the comment section in our podcast. The trolls won't just be angry about a missing episode, they'll be accusing me of hiding a real-life mystery.

Tick-tock, click-clack. What now? DONG, DONG! The grandfather clock in the formal living room is assaulting me. Wait, is it already ten?

Ding.

Dong.

Ping.

Buzz.

And now my phone won't stop going bananas in my pocket. I'm sure Nico and Emma are freaking out. I haven't gone this long without talking to them in, well, never.

Buzz.

Tick.

Scratch.

Write.

Ring.

Buzz.

I wish everyone and everything would just shut the hell up! I'm seriously about to lose it. The pain in my spine has moved up into my neck and settled in my head—it's a migraine. And unless you suffer like I do, then mind your own business. Because every noise, every little sound, every-stupid-thing is like a knife stabbing my frontal cortex.

Oh God! Why are the lights so bright? The room is spinning. I feel like I'm going blind and I'm probably going to puke. Maybe I should ask Mom to come over and hold her apron open for me.

I put my hands over my face and whisper through gritted teeth, "What was the question?"

"I said, do you know Gloria's other friends? The names of people we can contact? Her mother only gave us your name," tight-faced detective says, all judgy without any sort of empathy.

My eyes are closed but I can feel her frowning at me with her smooth, sour face. Followed by the two battle-ready officers snickering. That's it. I stand up and slam my hands on the table.

"I just told you—WE DON'T HANG OUT! Jesus. Get off my case already. I don't know a fucking thing about Gloria's disappearance."

"Grace Marie Everly," Mom yells at me. "Language!"

"Whaaaat? I have a horrible migraine, and I don't know anything. I want to go to bed," I whine, folding my arms and looking over my shoulder to pout at Mom.

"Well, officers, I think this has been enough for today. If Grace thinks of anything else, I'll call y'all immediately. Grace honey, I think you should go upstairs and lie down." Mom's southern accent is annoying and sweet. Like her tea. She rushes to my side and whispers, "Do you need one of your pills?" Her breath stinks.

Obviously, I need one of my pills.

"Pills?" the detective asks curiously while a hair-raising grin spreads across her face. Yuck. Who smiles at someone else's pain. The Grinch maybe?

"Yeah, I take prescription meds for my migraines, is that a crime?" I sneer, which sends shooting pains through my skull. Flashes of light. "Ohhh ughhhh..." I moan and put my hand up to my head and push my thumb between my eyes. Like if I push hard enough the part of my brain with the pain will burst out the back of my skull like popping some giant greasy pimple and give me some relief—

"Grace, no sweetheart, remember, don't push like that. It's not going to make the pain go away. Here, let me help you upstairs," Dad says and swoops in to play the hero, putting his massive, muscled arms around me and leading me upstairs before I can say something else shitty to the detective or drill a hole through my skull with my thumb.

I take a final look at her and she gives me an icy stare, like I'm a teen miscreant she'd love nothing more than to throw into juvenile detention for a week in solitary confinement.

But I am not a criminal.

Even if my house is full of cops.

I don't know anything about Gloria's disappearance!

"Detective Morgenson, I'm sorry for the confusion tonight. I don't think you quite understand. Gloria and Grace, they have a very strange friendship. I know it seems one-sided, but it works for them. I'm sorry Grace doesn't have more information to help you," Mom says, apologizing for my behavior. How irritating and cringeworthy. Whose side is she on anyway?

I think I did a fine job of explaining myself.

It's simple! I'm not friends with Gloria Sanchez. I don't have any information about what happened to her today. Period.

The voices downstairs are muffled by the time we get to the landing at the top of the stairs. Our cat hisses at me and skitters down the hall. Dad helps me to my bedroom and guides me to the bed. I collapse on my pile of blankets, thankful to be someplace soft. I roll over and grab my big stuffed dog pillow, Mr. Puppy. The one I've had forever. It's worn out and kind of junky, but I still love him. It's my migraine pillow. I bury my face into the fur and take a deep breath—I can still smell the bits of lavender Mom stitched into it when I was really little.

"How are you doing kiddo? This must be pretty scary, but you need to know, me and your mom won't let anything happen to you, okay? You're safe. There's going to be an officer posted outside our house until they find Gloria." Dad sits on my bed behind me and pats my shoulder with his huge hand, then dims the light on my nightstand.

"It's fine. I'm not scared, Dad. I'm more annoyed with everything." I lift my face up from my dog pillow. He hands me the stale glass of water off my nightstand and one of my migraine pills. After I swallow it and chug the glass of water I ask, "What did Mom mean when she said me and Gloria have a one-sided friendship? You guys know we aren't friends."

"Oh, you know how your mother is... And Grace," Dad adds, "no one blames you for any of this, so you don't have to worry, Detective Morgenson is just doing her job." He gets up and leaves my room, closing the door gently, probably afraid the noise will add to my migraine.

"God! Why would he fucking say that?" I yell at Mr. Puppy before burying my face deep into his squished saggy stuffing. Obviously, I'm not worried anyone blames me for Gloria being kidnapped today. I mean, for Christ's sake! I know I had nothing to do with it. We aren't friends! One-sided or two-sided. It's no-sided. We never talk. Well, she never talks.

Then I start crying.

Tears are coming out and I can't control them. Mr. Puppy is soaking them up, cradling my face like the good dog he is. Fucking Gloria. She's such a psycho! I mean, what was she thinking?

Ask Grace.

That's why the cops are at my house.

Ask Grace.

That's the only clue they have to go on.

Ask Grace.

She left a note on her desk this morning before school. Like she planned all of it from the very beginning. Like somehow she knew she'd get snatched from the school parking lot and wanted me to get blamed for it. What did I ever do to her? Seriously, what did I do? I mean, I wish someone would tell me what I did to deserve this.

<hr>

Chapter Two

WE AREN'T EVEN FRIENDS

We moved in next door to the Sanchez family when I was four. Dad's mixed-martial-arts gym concept blew up (not literally, figuratively... like he made a mint real fast). They call that *new money*. And with all that new money, my parents went on a spending spree. They wanted to get out of the scary apartments in Savannah and live in a perfect suburban neighborhood. You know, white picket fences and two-story houses, moms who stay home with their kids and drive a BMW or Range Rover and shop at the Publix instead of the Piggly Wiggly. We all have tennis lessons at the country club on Saturday and go to picnics after church on Sunday.

All that shit.

And what luck!

The Sanchezes had a little girl the exact same age as me. So boom, Mom and Dad shelled out all their new money to buy the dream. To give me the perfect life in the suburbs with a built-in best friend. But, much to their dismay, *Gloria hates me.*

I think it's because she's literally insane...

You know, mentally unstable.

I know this because:

A) Gloria is NOT audibly deficient. Yes, she speaks. I've heard her plenty of times. She talks to her parents. She talks at school. She answers teachers and sings in the show choir. Not to mention her lame attempts at flirting with this guy at school named Max. Which I have seen firsthand when she didn't know I was behind the door to the main office and she and Max were in the hallway. Her flirting is seriously tragic, by the way.

And B) I'm really not that bad to be around! I mean, I have friends. And a boyfriend. I'm like a totally well-adjusted, normal sixteen-year-old high school junior. There is seriously no reason for doll-faced tall-girl Gloria to ignore me.

But it's always been that way, since we were four years old.

I mean it—no lie.

Shut up! I'm not joking.

For as long as I've lived next to Gloria, she has never said a word to me. Not a laugh, not a snicker, not a "Hey Grace!", not a "You wanna hang after school?" or a "Let's get pizza and a movie! Or a sleepover?" Nothing. Nada. Zip. Zilch.

Like I said, it's fine.

I've grown used to being ignored by Gloria and even though she doesn't talk to me, sometimes—*okay most of the time*—I talk to her. What can I say? She's a good listener. It fills the black hole vortex of silence when we walk to school. Yeah sure, there are days I listen to K-pop on my headphones or text Nico and Emma about our obsession with *Stranger Things* or watch TikTok while we walk. But most of the time I blabber on and on to Gloria. I can't seem to help myself. The words just pour out of me like a raging river.

Look, you can stop judging me right now.

You don't know me!

I keep telling myself that one of these days I'm going to walk right past her house and not tell her it's time for school and just keep on walking without her. I'll fix this non-verbal problem by ignoring her. But without Gloria, what would my day feel like? My chest gets tight and my heart starts racing just thinking about it. There hasn't been a single day since we started school that Gloria and I didn't walk together. Rain or shine, like clockwork. I yell. She comes running out and jumps off the porch. Ugh, sometimes I even get her on the weekend and we go walk around the track at school.

But I will stop all of this right now if you don't get it through your thick skull that we are not friends. I'm serious! Me + Gloria = NOT FRIENDS!

I fall asleep and dream about the last time I saw Gloria, when we walked to school together. It's funny, because even in my dreams, I'm annoyed with her. There's this underlying tension that I've never been able to put my finger on. It's more than the no-talking thing. It's something else, scratching on the surface, aching to get out. But I don't know what it is—maybe Dream Me can figure it out.

"Gloria, come on, it's time for school." I put my hand up to my mouth and shout, even though I can see her through the screen door, putting her backpack on. I watch as Gloria gives her mom a big hug before she comes running out the door and leaps off the porch, landing in front of me. Like she always does. Her dark silky hair in that same stupid ponytail she's worn for as long as I can remember. It swings side to side from her goofy, over-the-top jump. I roll my eyes while she adjusts her backpack.

"So, what's new?" I ask.

Silence.

Gloria just stands there looking at me but not really seeing me, her head slightly cocked. Every day, it's the same shit with her; she comes running out of the house full of life with a smile the size of Texas, but the moment she jumps off the porch and our eyes meet, she becomes this statue. Stone-faced. But more like a vintage porcelain doll—because she's so pretty and super creepy. Whenever she's around me, she always wears a blank stare, one that I've tried a thousand times in the mirror to imitate but can never get just right. I always start laughing at myself. I really don't know how Gloria does it day after day, that blank face.

God she makes me so mad!

"Yeah, well, I've got a test in math, so don't bother telling me all your bullshit today, Gloria. I've got to have a clear mind, I don't need to hear all your drama," I say to her.

Silence.

I smile and laugh. "Yeah, that was pretty funny, wasn't it, Gloria. Well, are you ready for school?" I ask.

She doesn't respond. Surprise, surprise! So we start walking in silence. See, that thing about my math test, that actually was a joke. Because we both know two things.

First, I don't care about schoolwork, I have more important things to do with my time. Like singing K-pop karaoke and recording my podcast. So, me giving a crap about a math test, that's a laugh-worthy riot!

And second, Gloria is never going to bother me with incessant chatter. Because like I've been trying to tell you, Gloria hasn't said a word to me in years. Twelve years to be exact. But here we are, still walking to school together every day. It's strange and weird and totally psycho. My friends all think my parents make me walk with her, like some charity thing, you know, because Gloria isn't super popular or anything. I mean she's pretty and all, but she's like into nerdy stuff and she's kind of tall for a girl.

But my parents don't make me walk to school with Gloria.

I don't know… I guess I'm just used to her and that stupid ponytail.

I mean, if I didn't have Gloria to walk with, it just wouldn't feel normal. We've been doing it every single day of school for as long as I can remember. She's just part of my life—her and that porcelain doll face. Gloria and I have this bond, you can call it. Without her, I'm not sure I know who I really am. It's sick. I know.

"I said we aren't friends," I mumble in my sleep and jerk myself awake. I sit up in a panic. Looking around the dark. Worried. Nervous. "Ugh, Gloria." I flop back down on my pillow and try to go back to sleep, but instead I toss and turn. Like there's something sharp poking me in my bed.

God, she's a regular thorn in my side.

Chapter Three

Everyone Is So Annoying Today

"**Y**ou look like you didn't sleep at all last night. Are you okay?" my boyfriend Seth asks the next morning. He's waiting for me at the end of the driveway by the mailbox, black hair ruffled like he didn't get much sleep either. He's wearing that faded vintage Nirvana shirt I got him last year for his birthday and his hands are shoved in his pockets.

"I couldn't sleep after the cops left. I stayed up most of the night writing the next few episodes of the podcast." I don't want to tell him I was dreaming about Gloria. "How long have you been out here anyway? Why didn't you just come up to the house?" I ask and look around, my eyes darting, catching the mossy shadows in the oak trees.

"My dad just dropped me off a few minutes ago so I could walk with you," he answers. "Figured you didn't want to walk alone."

"Yeah, well you could have at least come up to the door to get me. Or are you still scared of my dad?" The wind blows my long hair in my face. I spin in the other direction and see Gloria's house. I should be walking over there to get her right now. Not standing here arguing with Seth at the end of my driveway.

There's a cop car parked across the street, just like Dad said there would be. Two officers sit inside, reading the paper and drinking coffee and eating donuts. Really? How cliché.

"I'm not scared of your dad. I'll even prove it—I'll go ask him if he can drive us to school." Seth puts his skinny arm around me.

"No!"

"What do you mean, no? After what happened yesterday, you really wanna walk?"

"Yes, asshole. This is MY three blocks." I push him away defensively. "I've walked to school every day since forever. And she didn't get kidnapped while we were walking to school."

"Right, it was after school," Seth says.

"No, it was during school. She left sixth period and went out to the parking lot, they have it on the school cameras. What's weird is the detective said they checked the cameras from all the surrounding businesses and traffic cameras and nothing. No sign of Gloria anywhere. It's like she disappeared into thin air. I mean, what are the odds?"

Seth scratches his head. He's trying to come up with the actual odds, like when he's playing Call of Duty and trying to decide how long he can last in the war zone. Who'd have thought I'd fall for such a nerdy gamer boy... But I mean, he fell for me too, right? All 115 pounds of K-pop-singing, podcast-recording, *Stranger Things*-obsessed me.

For a moment, I feel bad for calling him an asshole and pushing him away. I grab a handful of his shirt and pull him back to me. He stops calculating and smiles. I tug him closer, sucking in the smell of his leathery body spray before we kiss. Finally! A warm and happy feeling zings through my body, instead of all the angry bitterness I've been swimming in for the last twelve hours.

"Come on, let's go to school," I say when we finish kissing. I casually flip off the cops who are getting a free peep show. Then I grab Seth's hand and lace my fingers through his. He feels safe and his hands are a little clammy. God, I wish he lived next door to me instead of Gloria. My life would be a lot less dramatic that way.

We walk for a few moments, just swinging our hands, and for a split second I think everything is going to be okay. But then Seth has to go open his big fat mouth.

"I don't know Grace, I mean, you probably know her way better than anyone. Why would she leave sixth period like that? Did she tell you anything? Like was someone coming to pick her up? Have the cops tracked her phone or checked her social accounts or school email?" He asks all of this without taking a breath.

Ugh, he still wants to talk about Gloria?

"Oh my God. Are you for real? How many times do I have to tell you? Gloria doesn't talk to me." I try to walk faster and pull Seth's hand. That's one thing about Gloria, she has long legs and isn't afraid to use them. We usually make really good time on our walks to school. Not Seth, he's walking soooo slow and being super annoying. Okay, I change my mind. I could not do this with Seth every day.

"But what does that mean, Grace? I know you and Gloria never talk at school. I just figured you have different classes and shit," he says and shrugs. I can tell he's confused, which really pisses me off. I feel like I've had this conversation with him at least twenty times over the last year since we started dating.

"Uggggh."

He stops walking. "What? Don't roll your eyes and groan at me, Grace."

I can feel my blood pressure rising. "Seth! She literally, actually, for real never says a single word to me! For as long as I've known her, she hasn't spoken to me. Do you understand?" I let go of his hand and start speed walking at a pace even Gloria would have to hustle to keep up with.

I hear his feet slapping the pavement as he jogs to keep up with me. "Jesus, Grace," Seth complains, "why are you being such a bi—"

"Excuse me?" I spin around and cut him off before he can finish calling me a bitch. He comes to a screeching halt, nearly colliding with me.

"Sorry babe, that was uncalled for. I know you're hurting and confused. One of your best friends was kidnapped. I'm sorry." He's apologetic and backpedals hard. His cheeks blossom with pink and a bead of sweat forms on the edge of his dark ruffled hairline. Then he opens up his arms for a hug. I don't back away, but I also don't lean into him. He grins and leans forward, wrapping his arms around me. My face is buried in his chest. He's a lot taller than me.

"Yeah, it was uncalled for. You aren't allowed to call me names," I mumble into his chest. I can feel him nodding up and down. He might agree with me, but it doesn't mean I have to forgive him. So what if I'm pissed off? I have every right to be.

We walk the rest of the way to school in silence.

A sound I'm used to.

I can tell today is going to be super weird walking around the locker-lined halls of Richmond Hill High. No one is going to understand when I say I'm perfectly fine. Because if my own boyfriend thinks I'm best friends with Gloria, everyone else must think so too. God, how did I get myself into this mess? Just because we're next-door neighbors and walk together every day?

What about the note?

My brain keeps going back to that fact.

If that little bit of information gets out, there's no way I'll live it down… I shudder.

I pray to whatever deity is listening to please let that note remain a secret.

Ask Grace.

Goddamn Gloria. I'm really going to let her have it, whenever the cops do find her. Because I know they will find her. They have to, right? What the hell was she thinking anyway? Why did she leave sixth period in the middle of class and go out to the parking lot? Where could she have been going? I can't imagine she'd be meeting up with the losers who hang out behind the Kwik Stop vaping. I wonder if the cops even went over there to ask them? And why don't they have any footage of her from the cameras? There's one on the bank, one on the traffic light, one on the Kwik Stop. Hell, there's gotta be like ten in the school parking lot! Gloria might be a lot of things, but Invisible Woman is not one of them.

The hair on my arms prickles.

I mean, sure I'm obsessed with a show about a town where strange things happen, and me and my friends do a spoof podcast, making up fake mysteries about the woods around town, but there's no way any of it is real. There isn't a giant conspiracy to cover up Gloria being kidnapped. Richmond Hill doesn't have a government-run facility hiding a portal to an alternate universe in its basement. Okay, so sure, there's a big Army base not that far and we've all heard the loud explosions and seen the blue/green flares light up the night sky when they run ops. But it's nothing nefarious, like monsters and kidnapping; how gullible do you think I am?

"I'm sorry. Forgive me?" Seth asks outside the front doors to school.

"Fine." I reach up and let him give me a kiss. The bell rings and everyone rushes inside the building. I'm not ready to face it yet. I hesitate.

"Aren't you coming?"

"I think I'm gonna sit out here for a few minutes, you know, collect my thoughts before I go in."

I watch him go into school, and I walk over to one of the live oak trees near the parking lot and sit down, leaning my back against its bark. I stare up at the Spanish moss waving in the breeze. Sunlight filters through the leaves and moss, making little patterns of light. It reminds me of the podcast me and Nico recorded a few months ago when Emma was at a soccer tournament out of town.

I pop in my headphones and search through my phone for the episode. Usually I hate listening to myself, but I don't want to go into school yet, and I don't want to sit here in silence. The sound of my voice is strange... I close my eyes, thinking about me and Nico sitting in her dark closet to record, the glow from my laptop illuminating our faces.

ME: *Welcome to another episode of—*

NICO (using her ominous voice): *What's in the Woods?*

ME: *The podcast that will scare your socks off.*

NICO: *Really Grace? Scare your socks off?*

ME: *Shut up Nico. What should I say? Scare the piss out of you?*

NICO (laughing uncontrollably): *Only you would say something like that. A-n-y-way... this episode is about Alice Riley, the first convicted murderer in the new world. Alice's death condemned her to life as a ghost, and she's forever searching Savannah, looking for her missing baby.*

ME: *Oh yeah, the one tourists say comes up to strollers, like a flash of sparkly light. Soooo, I'm dying to know, who'd she kill? And who stole her baby?*

NICO: *Well, as the story goes, she killed this old disgusting rich dude, who made her brush his long, greasy, old man hair every day. He was bedridden, which means she was probably wiping his butt, not just brushing his hair.*

ME: *Yuck! I'd probably kill him too. Why was she even there? Why didn't she just run away?*

NICO: *She couldn't. She was trapped, as his servant. He'd paid for her voyage from Ireland. So I guess she owed him. Plus, she had the baby.*

ME: *Babies are the worst.*

NICO (snorting, trying not to laugh): *The baby didn't go missing until after she was dead. Some reports say the baby crawled off into the woods, in search of his mother. Some say it was the man Alice killed; his ghost came back to kidnap it as revenge.*

ME: *Ew, what if it was his baby!*

ME and NICO at the same time shrieking and hissing: *GROSS!!*

I remember being super nauseated when we did that episode. Like it triggered a memory. Talking about a woman being trapped against her will in a life of servitude to a creepy old man. Imagining his wrinkly, crusty hands as they stretched out to touch poor Alice, how she must have felt. Knowing her spirit roamed these parts in search of her missing baby—

Someone shakes my shoulder.

I scream. My eyes fly open. I'm completely disoriented. I forgot I was even at school and now I'm staring at Mr. Jones, the assistant principal.

"Miss Everly, sorry to startle you, but I'm gonna need you to head to class," he says and offers a hand to me. My heart is still banging against my rib cage when I take his hand and let him pull me to my feet.

"You shouldn't sneak up on people like that." I look Mr. Jones in the eyes.

He quickly looks away, before saying, "Don't worry, they'll find her."

"Who? Alice's ghost?" I'm so confused. Did he hear the podcast?

"The police will find your friend Gloria. Now, you better hurry up, first period is almost over."

Oh. Gloria. And I was just starting to forget about that entire thing.

***

"Grace, how are you holdin' up?" Mrs. Kelley asks as I walk into my first class. She follows me to my orange plastic seat and gives me her best sad face as I take off my backpack and sling it on the chair.

"I'm fine," I grumble and slump down. She looks like she's going to say more, but the rest of the class gets loud and she rushes back to the front to get things under control, saving me from her unnecessary sympathy.

And so it begins. All day. Everywhere I turn. Teachers with big round eyes. Everyone in class patting my shoulder or trying to hug me as I make my way down the aisle.

"Don't worry Grace, they're gonna find her."

"Oh Grace! You must be so worried!"

"We are here for you, Grace."

"Prayer circle for Gloria after school—Grace, you should be there."

I'm really trying to keep my cool. Seriously, I am! See—I have a smile. Okay, I have an extremely strained smile, but it's still there. I'm taking a big deep breath in through my nose and out through my fake, weirdly toothy grin. Ew! I put my hand over my mouth. What is wrong with me?

But honestly, if I hear one more word about Gloria, I will freak the hell out. Thank God I'm in Mr. Creed's history class and he doesn't make you ask to use the bathroom, you can just get up and go. I slip out the back of the classroom as soon as he dims the lights and turns on a movie about the Roman Empire.

The halls are empty and I run into the closest bathroom.

"Finally, someplace quiet," I say after I check under all the stalls to make sure there aren't any freshmen hiding out. I look in the mirror and try to imitate the face Gloria makes. Pouty lips. Big wide eyes. Very Wednesday Adams. Then I stick my tongue out at my reflection and laugh before looking myself up and down. I've got on my favorite gray joggers and striped, blue-and-orange crop shirt and the black hoodie I got for my birthday. Yeah, I know this is Georgia and it's hot as hell, but they keep the school a cool sixty-two degrees to make us stay awake. A sweatshirt is a must!

I pull my dark coppery hair forward and smooth it out. It's long, down to my waist. Mom keeps bitching at me to cut it, but she doesn't understand this is the style. Unless you want me to put it in a stupid ponytail, like *you-know-who*. I lean in close and pick at a pimple that's forming near the side of my nose. I forgot to use my acne meds last night. Stupid cops. Stupid Gloria.

I feel completely out of my normal routine and I don't like it at all. I'm a creature of habit.

I hear a sound outside the bathroom, and the door creaks as someone begins to push it open, so I duck into a stall—careful to pull the laminate door as quiet as I can, sliding the flat silver lock before they can hear me. I don't want to deal with anyone right now.

Two, maybe three, girls walk in laughing.

Just as long as it's not Dani and Zane... I hate those girls. They are so mean all the time. To everyone, not just me in particular.

"Oh shut up Dani, you don't know anything," says a familiar voice.

Zane Holden. My nemesis. With her perfect teeth and perfect manners. More like perfect bullshit. I know she's the one using the tag 7TRUTHZ to troll on our podcast. She leaves the strangest comments—they are so unoriginal, more like famous quotes she copies off the internet, and all oddly religious.

"I'm serious, Zane! You know my older brother Peter is an intern at the police department! He said Grace Everly knows what happened to Gloria, but she's refusing to tell them. The cops are watching her house—you know, for clues," Dani Kerst says matter-of-factly, and then gets her hot pink lip gloss out of her bag.

My heart starts racing and I step back from where I was watching through the crack in the door, but I can still see them well enough as Zane pushes Dani.

"You're such a liar!" Zane yells, her blonde hair bouncing when Dani pushes her back. They laugh. God, how annoying and perfect their little banter is. I want to rip my hair out.

So the cops do actually think I know what happened to Gloria and now everyone at school is going to think so too if Zane and Dani have their way. I oughta march out of this stall and smack them both in the face. But of course I'm mostly talk, no real game. No matter how many times my dad has begged me to train at his gym, I always find a way out of it. It's been years since I've put on a pair of boxing gloves and punched out my feelings.

"Wait, I'm confused. Why do the cops think Grace had something to do with Gloria's disappearance? Me and Gloria are in choir together... She said Grace is her best friend. I mean, they walk together every single day and have grown up next door to each other." That's Sarah Gideon. I really don't know why she hangs with Zane and Dani. They suck and she's kind of nice. We hung out a few times in sixth grade before she switched to the dark side.

"No, stupid, they don't think Grace had something to do with Gloria's disappearance. They think Gloria ran away or something and Grace is covering for her!" Dani steps back from the mirror and looks over her shoulder at the stall I'm in. I quickly flush the toilet and cough a few times. And flush again.

"Ew, gross! A pooper!" They all laugh. "Come on, let's go!"

"If either of you bitches ever try to run away, I am not covering for you," Zane teases and they all laugh again and pile out the bathroom door.

Do the cops really think Gloria ran away and that I'm covering for her? That's insanity! I wouldn't cover for her if my life depended on it. Running away is what losers do. I carefully open the stall and peek out, just to make sure Zane, Dani, and Sarah are actually gone. There's a little ache in my heart. No, not an ache—more like a tug. Why would Gloria tell Sarah I'm her best friend?

I shake my head. Maybe I misunderstood.

I can't wait to tell Nico and Emma about this! Speaking of my *real friends*, I haven't seen them today; why haven't they been around?

Rushing back to history class, my head is spinning as I slip into my cold plastic seat without so much as a glance from Mr. Creed. Quickly, I text Emma and Nico in our group chat, demanding to know if they are at school today, and wait a few seconds.

No response. Thankfully, it's almost lunch, and Emma, Nico, and I have the same bell schedule and sit together every day. The bell rings and Mr. Creed flicks on the lights. We all rush in a mass for the door, this time no one is asking if I'm doing all right, since they all just want to get to lunch. The smell of lunchroom mystery meat is heavy in the air.

"Miss Everly, wait, for a moment," Mr. Creed says as I'm already halfway out. I pause, but don't turn around. I swear if he says anything about Gloria...

"Yes, sir?" I finally turn and face him.

"I just wanted to make sure you're hanging in there, you know, because of what happened yesterday. If there is anything the staff here can do, you just have to let us know," he says as kindly as he can. And even though I want to scream at him right now, I don't.

"I'm fine," I reply, but the hair raises on my arm again.

Something feels off and I don't know what it is.

Like everyone knows something that I don't.

"Well, if you need to talk, I'm here," Mr. Creed says and pats my shoulder.

Fat chance.

I rush to the lunchroom and wade through the stench of dried0out meat loaf mixed with teenage BO to find Seth, Emma, and Nico. I see them at our usual table, the farthest one by the window.

"Today is a weird day," Nico says around a mouthful of her usual PB&J sandwich. Her jet-black hair is pulled into two braids on either side of her head and there are Hello Kitty hair clips and beads pinned all over in no particular order. She's wearing a neon yellow dress with a cute patchwork jacket and some seriously tall white platform lace-ups. I might be the leader of our friend group, but Nico is definitely the fashion trendsetter. I could never pull off that look.

I set my bag on the table and rest my chin on it. "Weird is an understatement," I moan. I'm half-tempted to start rambling about Gloria, but then I'd be no better than everyone else who has annoyed me today. I know Nico and Emma *aren't* asking me about it for that very reason.

"Grace, get some food." Emma nudges me.

"I can't eat right now." I close my eyes. I'm still kinda mad at Seth from this morning, and I don't want to look at his face. He usually sits next to me at lunch, but today he swapped with Emma and is sitting across from me. He's keeping his mouth shut—or rather, stuffed with Flamin' Hot Cheetos.

So I just listen, not to his crunching, but to my friends as they talk.

"Are we recording the new episode tonight, since we missed last night?" Nico asks.

"Umm... don't kill me guys, but I never finished my part of the script," Emma admits.

I keep my head down but raise my hand up and groan. "I finished it on the shared drive, and I wrote the next few episodes. I couldn't sleep."

"Way to go Grace, working through your, uh, stress about..." Nico laughs nervously and doesn't finish whatever she was about to say. I'm sure it had something to do with Gloria.

"I'll be over as soon as I can get out of soccer practice, so don't start recording without me." Emma nudges me again and I glance up at her. Her short purple hair is swooped to one side and starting to seriously fade.

"I'm gonna walk home with you, Grace," Nico says. "I brought my gear to school, figured you'd, uh, need me."

I lift my head up from my bag and look at my friends just in time to see Nico put another bite of sandwich in her mouth. I frown at her.

"Wh-a-aaaat?" Her voice is peanut-butter muffled. "All this shit about Gloria is freaking me out. I'm stress-eating."

I raise an eyebrow at her.

"I'm coming over too. Like around eight—after my guitar lessons." Seth decides to finally speak up after he's done licking the bright red Cheeto dust off his fingers.

"No," I tell him.

"And why not?" he asks.

"Because we have to record our podcast. You're a distraction. But you can come over tomorrow and hang out with me, if you want," I suggest. He nods and pulls out a piece of paper from his bag and starts writing. I don't have to look at it to see it's his math homework. He answers the problems faster than I'd even be done reading the instructions. Seth is like a mathematical genius, in addition to being a gamer. But he's never been very good about managing his time. I stare at his pencil as it slides across the pages, lost in mindless thoughts, trying not to think about Gloria. I look over my shoulder, to the table she usually sits at with the girls from choir. The table is empty. I wonder where they all are?

The bell rings and I startle. Has it seriously been twenty-five minutes? My head is not in the game. I stand up slowly and Seth walks around the table as Emma and Nico scatter to their next classes. I shout goodbye, but my voice is drowned out in the crowd.

"Are you still mad at me from this morning?" He wraps his arms around me. He smells spicy and even though I want to be mad, I melt into him. He feels my body sinking and he squeezes me harder.

"No, I'm not really mad. I guess I just need Emma and Nico tonight. Honestly, I wasn't worried about this thing with Gloria until right now—I can tell Nico and Emma are freaked out. All my teachers are being weird. I don't understand why everyone here thinks I should be so broken up about her going missing," I complain.

"Um, because, Grace—don't you think you're being sort of heartless? Like, it's okay to admit that you liked Gloria." Seth lets me have it. "It's okay to say she was your best friend. So what if you didn't talk? Wait—I mean *she* didn't talk. You guys were still friends. Closer than any of us who wander these halls alone all day. Just admit it and deal with your feelings."

"You know what Seth, you don't know a fucking thing, do you?" I sneer. Then I push him away from me and storm off to my next class. Seriously, who does Seth think he is? He doesn't know anything! Especially about me and Gloria.

Chapter Four

THE BIG BAD DREAM

After school, I run to the edge of the sidewalk where all the walk-ers leave campus, expecting to see my tall ponytailed goofball Gloria waiting to walk home with me. I have so much to tell her! My heart sinks when I remember she's not going to be there. And then I get mad at myself, because ugh, God, Gloria is so annoying! Why do I have this stupid need to be with her every day?

Thankfully, someone else familiar is standing in Gloria's place waiting for me. "Hey babes!" Nico opens up her arms for a hug.

"Hey girl." I walk up and rest my head on her shoulder and let her hug me. I'm glad I have friends I can lean on. Literally. I've got my full weight on Nico and she's holding steady.

"So, you gonna tell me the truth?" She looks deep in my eyes and asks when I finally take a step back from our hug. "My bro said cops were at your place last night and there was one camped in front of your house this morning."

I shrug and let out a sigh as we start walking. It takes half a block before I finally look over at her and say anything.

"Your brother needs to stop spying on me." It's not that I don't think her brother Kevin is cute and all, but he's a freshman and we're juniors. He's had this big stupid crush on me for forever and is always riding his bike past my house. He's lucky Seth isn't the jealous, beat-a-younger-kid-up type. Actually, Seth befriended Kevin and now they play video games together all the time. Eye roll.

"Yeah, yeah, Kevin is a little troll. But is it true? Were there cops at your house last night *and* this morning?"

I nod. "A couple of cops and a detective with a stick up her ass. She wanted to know if I knew anything about Gloria's disappearance."

"No shit!" Nico shakes her head.

"Yeah, her mom had the nerve to tell them that we're best friends. Which seriously pisses me off, considering we aren't friends. Not even close!" Color rises in my cheeks just thinking about it. I mean, seriously, who does Mrs. Sanchez think she is? Telling that detective me and Gloria are best friends.

Nico grabs my arm and stops walking. "Grace, why you gotta lie to me? Huh? I used to think your parents made you walk with her—cause you know, the buddy system—when y'all were little, but I know you. You never do anything you don't want to do. You're a very intentional person. So, seriously, what's the deal with you and Gloria?"

Ask Grace. The note is screaming.

"Look. There's something you should know." But I honestly don't know if I should tell her about the note.

Ask Grace. Louder.

"I knew it!" Nico shouts.

Ask Grace. So loud I can hardly hear myself think.

"You knew what, Nico?" I'm exasperated. Between Nico and the note.

"You're friends with her."

"We aren't friends, I just—we've walked together every day. I'm used to her, that's all." My voice is soft and defeated.

"Oh." Nico pats my shoulder. "Look, it's okay, whatever she means to you."

"There is something else. I just don't know if I'm supposed to tell you." Maybe I'm supposed to keep it a secret. It is evidence after all. But if the cops really think I'm covering up Gloria running away, like Dani told Zane in the bathroom, then why are they wasting resources by having cops parked outside my house? It doesn't make any sense. None of this makes any sense. My head is swimming.

I pull out my phone and dial a number before Nico can ask me what I'm hiding. A number that I have for emergencies. I mean, Mrs. Sanchez has had to pick up me and Gloria on more than one occasion when we've had those thunderstorms with rain so hard you can't see a foot in front of your face. She answers on the first ring and I hit the speaker button so Nico can listen.

"Hey Mrs. Sanchez—how are you doing? Any word about Gloria?" I ask. God, how much easier would this all be if she said, *why yes, Gloria is sitting right here next to me, they found her at the mall shopping.*

"No, Grace, nothing yet," she says sadly. "I'm glad you called, sweetheart. I know how hard this must be on you. How was it at school today?"

I let out a long sigh. "Uh, okay, I guess… But weird without Gloria."

She doesn't say anything. There's a sound like a sniffle.

"Um, would it be all right if I brought Nico over and we looked at the note Gloria left on her desk? I mean, if the cops didn't take it last night."

Nico looks totally confused.

She mouths, *"What note?"*

"Yes, of course you girls can come over. The note is still there where Gloria left it. The police took some pictures…" her voice trails off and she sighs. "They weren't even here very long." I can hear the disdain in her voice. I don't blame her. They spent hours harassing me last night and only a few minutes at Gloria's house? What gives?

"I honestly don't know what the note is about, Mrs. Sanchez, but I thought if I looked at it, maybe it would—" I pause. I'd fully expected her to tell me no, so I had this whole spiel prepared, but now that feels out of place. "Thanks. See you soon." I quickly hang up.

"Um, girl, what the hell was that about?" Nico asks.

"You'll see. Come on." I grab Nico's hand and we run the rest of the way. Which isn't easy since she's wearing platforms. Her black braids bounce, threatening to spill Hello Kitty barrettes all over the sidewalk. I don't know how those little things stay in her hair like that.

I haven't been over to Gloria's house in years. I used to go over there every Friday night in elementary school—our parents played cards in the dining room. They would make us popcorn and candy and rent movies. Gloria sat silently on the couch and I'd do flips and somersaults and bounce around and talk through most of the movie until I passed out. But then I got old enough for sleepovers with Nico and Emma and stopped going over to the Sanchezes' on Friday nights. And after a while, Mom and Dad stopped going too. I guess they finally realized they couldn't force a friendship. I mean, seriously, what were they thinking?

We trudge up the front porch and ring the bell. I'm sweating, because I'm nervous. I mean, for fuck's sake, Gloria the sociopath walked off and got kidnapped from school and I haven't been inside her house in years and I don't know if she's got skulls and crossbones hanging on her walls, or weird shit, or—

"Grace!" Mrs. Sanchez exclaims when she opens the door. She looks tired and clearly she's been crying, but she puts on a smile for us. "And Nico! Nice to see you dear, you've gotten so tall. I don't know if you remember, you've been here a few times for movie night—oh, maybe back when you girls were in fifth or sixth grade?"

"Hi. Oh yeah, I forgot about that." Nico smiles back. I'd forgotten about that too.

A sharp pain shoots up my leg, zips like fire through my spine and out through my left eye. Oh no, if I'm about to get another migraine, I might seriously lose my shit. They've been coming more frequently than ever before. Especially when I think about things from my past, like my memories of being a kid don't want to be relived or something.

"Grace, you know where Gloria's room is. Just head on up." Mrs. Sanchez waves her hand and motions us into the house. It's the same as I remember once we get inside. Very tidy, like a page out of *Southern Living* magazine. It's actually a lot like our house. Probably because Mom and Mrs. Sanchez used to hang out and shop together all the time. "I'll be in the kitchen, making you girls a snack!" she shouts after us as Nico and I take off our shoes and run up the carpeted stairs.

I feel guilty being here without Gloria. I've never been here without her. I'd be so angry if she was snooping around my room without me. And look at me—about to do it to her.

Nico pushes her door open without any concern.

I hold onto the doorjamb to brace myself for what we are about to see. I expect next-level kind of horror shit. Because deep down it's Gloria who must be the horrible person to spend twelve years never speaking to me. Maybe she's a satanist or a witch and the room will be filled with shrunken heads and glass bottles bubbling with potions and frogs and severed fingers.

"Ah, her room is so nice," Nico says cheerfully from within the tomb of demon Gloria. "God, I really hope she's okay. I mean, it's pretty screwed up that someone kidnapped her." Her tone saddens almost instantly.

I can't answer.

Because I'm not prepared as I cross the threshold. My heart is racing. My palms are sweaty. What is wrong with me? Why did I imagine it would be like the devil's playground? Because it is nothing like that.

It looks like what I remember from when we were little kids. Pale lavender walls, white trim, soft curtains framing the two big windows on either side of her bed. The bed is bigger, the child-sized twin replaced with a queen. It's covered with white-and-gold polka-dot bedding. There are some Chinese paper lanterns hanging in the corner in various shades of blue and violet. And on one wall there are some black-and-white pictures of her and her parents on vacation at the beach and camping, surrounded by tall trees. Above her desk is a photo board filled with more pictures of her and the girls from Show Choir.

"She's totally normal. Tell me again why we never hang out with Gloria?" Nico asks, picking up a pink furry stuffed unicorn off her bed and holding it in her arms. She cradles it like it's something special.

"Because—hello!" Now I'm angry all over again. "She never ever talks to me. This is so fake! How can she be so normal?" I'm flustered and jealous or something. I mean, why couldn't Gloria just talk to me? What did I do that was so terribly wrong that she had to completely ignore me, never talk, never laugh, never smile or act like I was worthy of her friendship?

Because she's a fucking psycho.

That's why!

Maybe she doesn't have black walls and a cauldron, but she's evil. Only a mean, evil person would treat someone the way she treats me.

"Look, this is why we are here." I huff and puff and march over to her desk against the far wall. And there, sitting on the middle of it, like no one has even touched it, is the note. Come on Richmond Hill cops! Why didn't they bag this for evidence? I point at it, waiting for Nico to look. She leans over the desk.

"Ask Grace." Nico reads the words out loud.

She picks up the paper and turns it over in her hands a few times, then glances around the rest of the desk, for other clues I suppose. After a minute she spins around, her face completely serious. "Grace, do you know what happened to Gloria?"

I laugh, one loud high-pitched anxious sound. Like I'm disgusted. Or nervous.

I suck in a deep breath and smell Gloria in the air. It envelops me, like a warm wind on the beach at Tybee Island. I can hear Gloria laughing... but not her teenage laugh, the one I sometimes hear at school when she doesn't know I can hear her. This is a child's laugh.

Grace, come build a sandcastle with me! The words, plain as day. Gloria spoke to me. There's no way for it not to be a memory, it's too real inside my head.

A really weird fuzzy feeling takes over me. I grab onto the white desk chair and hold on, because for a second I feel like I'm going to fall over. What is happening? My head starts pounding.

"Are you okay?" Nico puts her hand on my shoulder to steady me.

"Um, I don't know, I could have sworn I just heard Gloria talking to me, like a memory from when we were kids. I think I need to sit down—" But before I can get myself in the desk chair or on the bed, my knees buckle and I fall to the floor.

"GRACE!" Nico screams. "Mrs. Sanchez, come quick, something is wrong!" Nico shouts. "Grace, you're okay, I'm right here."

The world is spinning around me.

"I, uh, water?" My lips form words, but they feel clunky and awkward in my mouth. Before I can say anything else, I feel my eyes roll into the back of my head. And suddenly I'm gone.

I'm so far from this place, this room, this entire world.

I'm just gone.

Chapter Five

THE TRUTH IN BITS AND PIECES

I open my eyes, expecting to be on the floor in Gloria's room. But I'm somewhere else entirely. I look down at myself... I'm uh, okay, this is really weird to say, but I think I've gone back in time. I'm practically a toddler. Look at these chubby little hands! Then, before I know what I'm doing, I start shushing someone.

"Shhhhh..." I whisper.

"Grace, I'm scared," Gloria whimpers. She's sitting in the corner of a dark metal cage.

A flash of recognition crosses my brain. We've been living here for the last week. The man with the rotten-looking face is about to leave; I can tell because he's put on an orange hunting vest and a pair of boots. He only leaves for one reason.

Food.

"I'll protect you, Gloria. Mommy says I'm brave," I remind her softly. And I AM brave. I'm strong from soccer. I'm strong from swimming. My muscles yearn to be free from this cramped, smelly, icky place we've been locked in like dogs.

As if they sense I was thinking about them, or maybe because their owner is leaving, the puppies all start whining and clawing at their own cages. Their activity alerts the rotten-faced man and he turns sharply to stare down the whiners.

"Shut up, you little pissers," he yells at the puppies. Gloria and I back as far into our cage as we can. We push our small bodies against the cold metal frame, ignoring the feces on the floor. It's better to be as far back as possible. Let the real dogs get the attention.

But his voice just makes them cry louder instead of shutting them up. They are hungry. He doesn't feed any of us enough food. "Yip!" barks the little brown and white one a few cages down.

"Shut up, idiot." The man approaches. I'm frantic he's going to hurt it again. Poor little puppy. One of its eyes is gone. The man hurts the puppies. But I'm a brave girl. I'm not going to cry; I don't want him to hurt me and Gloria.

He limps forward. That leg, the left one—something is wrong with it. He can't move very fast. But he manages to bend over and he puts his fingers into the cage of the yipper. "Gotta go pick up hot dogs. Maybe I'll turn you ugly piece of shit into a hot dog." He laughs and coughs and burps all at once and it's so yucky. I try not to throw up.

Gloria is shaking and I wrap my arms around her and hold her tightly. "Shhh... just think about the beach, and building sandcastles," I tell her. Going to the beach with Gloria is one of my favorite things to do. She's the best sandcastle builder on the entire beach. She knows how to build a moat and fill it with water and seashells.

"You two mutts, you want some lunch when I get back? Maybe I'll cook up a little hot dog for you, or one of these pissers!" He laughs and kicks the cages. Poor little puppies. They all cry. I bite my lip and try not to cry because my tummy hurts. Just the mention of eating food, even with the yucky smells and being locked in this cage, makes me want to scream out, like a seagull diving in for our picnic basket. But we know we have to stay quiet.

I close my eyes and try to block out the man. I miss my mommy and peanut butter and jelly and milk and cookies and French fries.

"It's okay Grace, he's gone," Gloria whispers. Now she's the one holding me. I'm shaking so bad. Big salty tears run down my face and into my mouth. They taste like the ocean. "Grace, Grace…"

"Grace." Someone is shaking my shoulder.

"GRACE!"

"NO!" I shriek. "I don't want a hot dog!" I am frantic. Panicked. Oh God. Holy shit.

I blink a few times. "Huh?" I moan. Oh man, my head is pounding and my brain is slamming side to side. I'm about to throw up, but then I remember where I am. Gloria's bedroom. I don't want to throw up in her room, that would be rude. Right? What an insane made-up dream that was.

"Ugh, that was so gross," I whine.

"Grace, are you okay?" Nico asks, her breath tickling my nose because she's hovering right over me.

"Jesus, Nico, why are you so close to my face?" I push myself back and sit against the edge of Gloria's bed.

"You were having a seizure or something! Don't be such a bitch!" Nico exclaims.

"First of all, what is it with everyone calling me a bitch today? And second, I don't have seizures. I have a migraine. My head—it's—I need my meds. Can you get my mom?" I manage to squeak out. I'm really sick of my friends and boyfriend accusing me of being a bitch today. Like for real, I mean, this has been a seriously strange twenty-four hours. Cut me some slack, okay? And I'm not in the mood for any of this.

Crazy dreams. Seizures. Migraines.

Missing neighbor girls who annoy the shit out of me.

"Mrs. Sanchez ran to get your mom. I thought you were having a seizure, like for real! You were standing there and then your eyes rolled into the back of your head and you fell to your knees and passed out," Nico is talking fast. I can tell she's freaked out. I mean, I guess I would be too. But I don't have seizures. I think I'm just stressed out about this whole Gloria thing and that she left a message with my name on it. As if I'm supposed to know what happened to her. Which, clearly, I don't know what happened to her, even if I just had some sicko dream about us as kids locked in a cage, puke!

"Look, I'm fine. It's just my head. I need my meds and a glass of water. I'm fine, relax." I rub my hands over my face and swoop my long hair back from my neck.

Nico takes out her phone. She's uncomfortable. That's what she does, buries her nose in her phone when she doesn't know what to say.

"What time is Emma coming over?" I ask, trying to change the subject.

"She said as soon as she's done with practice her mom will drop her off at your house. Since you're awake, can we go to your house now?" Nico starts pacing around Gloria's room.

"You can go. I need my mom to help me." I'm nervous to walk on my own, since my body feels like Jello and I don't want my knees to buckle.

"Grace! Grace!" Mom is shouting. I can hear her running up the stairs. She barges into Gloria's room. "Jesus, are you okay?" She's frantic.

"I'm okay, Mom, relax," I reply. Even though I'm not really sure if I am okay. I mean, what the hell was that dream all about? With that super gross burn-victim-looking man and all the dogs and being in a cage with Gloria. And she spoke to me. It felt soooo painfully real. It was strange and true in a way a dream has never felt to me before.

I shiver.

"Grace, oh, sweetheart!" Mom is crouched down next to me and trying to hug me. Her presence makes my head hurt and I flinch and lean away from her.

"God, Mom, back off! I just want to go home. Emma's coming over when she's done with practice and this place is freaking Nico out too. I mean, look at her."

"Uh, what?" Nico looks up from her phone.

"Okay girls. Enough of this. Let's get you back to our house for your sleepover," Mom says way too cheerfully considering what has happened. "Nico, you lead the way. Daisy, thanks for letting the girls come over. I'm sorry for all the trouble. Call me later, okay?" Mom says to Gloria's mom who is shifting from one foot to the other. She looks terrible. Like she's seen a ghost. Her face is pale white and her eyes are black. Ew, she looks dead like Morticia Addams. Maybe that's where Gloria gets it from.

"Everything is going to be fine," Mom whispers and then uses some kind of crazy mom power to pick me up off the floor and cradle me to her body. I don't fight her. I go limp and put my head on her shoulder.

I'm not sure why, but I can't seem to wrap my head around what just happened. I keep seeing the burned-up face of that man and hearing Gloria whimper in the dog cage. And then everything goes black, again.

Oh great.

This is getting really annoying...

***

"Grace," little-kid Gloria hisses and shakes my shoulder.

"No," I snarl at her and curl my body into the smallest little ball, resting my head on the crook of my arm.

Doesn't she know the man with the rotten face will come back again if we are too loud? He'll put that pointy stick through the cage and poke us until we cry. He'll laugh and howl and keep poking until we can't cry anymore. We have to be quiet. It's dark outside. This is his sleeping time. But Gloria is so annoying. She keeps hissing and tugging on me and moaning like she has to go potty.

"Use the bucket," I whisper.

"No. I don't have to go potty. I heard the truck leave," she says softly into my ear.

Oh my God. This is it!

She doesn't have to tell me twice. I uncurl from my ball and crawl over to the edge of the cage, just like we practiced when he goes outside wearing the orange vest. The orange vest means he'll be gone for a long time.

The truck means he'll be gone for even longer.

"The keys," she hisses.

I reach my hand through the metal bars of our dog cage. Gloria holds it steady with her chubby little hands so it doesn't rattle and wake up the puppies in their cages. Once they start barking and growling and crying, there's no stopping them. My heart is pounding.

Gloria is doing her best not to whimper. She's really picked up some bad habits here. She's practically a dog these days! It's so dark that I can't see what I'm doing; I just have to feel for the edge of the wall with the flaking paint. There is a row of hooks where the man hangs the keys. He keeps them close, so it's easy to let us go potty outside. But mostly he makes us and the other puppies go in our cages.

He's a very bad pet owner.

I don't even know why he has all of us here.

He mostly just yells at us, pokes us with that stick, and threatens not to feed us. But deep down inside my tummy, it feels wrong. Like any day, any moment, he might yank one of us, me or Gloria or the puppies, out of the cage and take us into the woods and we'd never come back. He's a monster. A terrible, horrible, scary-faced monster.

The collar around my neck feels so tight I want to rip it off. Tears are rushing down my cheeks and my arm is losing feeling because I'm pushing it so hard to get it out of the cage and up the wall. Gloria makes a teensy tiny little sound in her throat. It's enough to make me remember we have to get the keys if we want to escape and I wedge my shoulder just a little further.

Finally I feel the metal of the keys on the hook, the one in the middle. Gloria was right! My arm is long enough! With a final push my shoulder blade unhinges and my hand grasps the keys. I bite my lip from the pain, tasting salty blood in my mouth. But I don't cry. I'm a brave girl. I'm Mommy's big, super-duper helper. And big girls don't cry.

I clasp the keys, turning them once to the left, enough for the ring to come off the hook without making any noise, and slowly pull my arm back into the cage. I'm very, very careful. Because if they fall out of my hands and hit the floor and wake up all the puppies, that's the end of this. The man will know we tried to escape if he comes home and hears them barking and sees the keys on the floor.

And we know what happens to little girls who try to escape from the man.

They get the shock collar.

I should know. He put one on me a few days ago, when we tried to run out while he was cleaning our cage. The shock was more painful

than when I fell in the gravel by Daddy's work and split my knees and
hands open.

As soon as my arm is back inside the cage with the keys, I turn my
neck to Gloria. I don't even have to ask. She makes quick work of it
and removes my shock collar. Her collar is already off, on the floor of
our cage.

We have the keys.

Time to run for our lives.

Chapter Six

SOUTHERN FRIED THERAPY

"**N**OOOOOO!" I scream and sit up in my bed. I'm panting and sweating and my heart feels like it's going to explode out of my chest because it is beating way too fast.

"Grace, take a deep breath. You're in your own home, in your own bed." It's a voice I haven't heard in a while.

"Oh... Tammy. What are you doing here?" I ask and open my eyes to a slit. I half expect to see Tammy sitting on the foot of my bed. Which would be seriously annoying. Instead, it's just me. Alone in my room. "Where is everyone?" I say and look around.

"Downstairs," Tammy says from the computer screen. Mom must have left her laptop open, sitting on my nightstand. God, Mom. Really? Leaving Tammy there to watch me sleep? I mean, kind of creepy.

"How long have you been watching me sleep?" I pick up the laptop and look at Dr. Tammy Michaels. She's Mom's cousin and she is always so fucking happy. With that bouncy blonde hair and those warm blue eyes. Look at her smile. Pink lipstick, perfectly white teeth. She's like a model for a southern dating app. I just can't with her right now...

A flash of rotten-face man blinds me momentarily and I involuntarily cringe and gag. "Sorry," I mumble to excuse my facial tick.

She ignores it. "To answer you, I've not been watching you for long, Grace. Your mom and I were talking and she had to set the laptop down. Something about a pizza delivery," Tammy says.

I ignore her and get up to turn on my bedroom light and da-ta-da-daaaa my migraine is gone! I can stand without my knees shaking and feeling like I'm going to pass out. Phew! Because I swear, any more of that passing-out crap, and I might start punching things out of rage. My stomach growls. A good sign. Food always does me a world of good. I can hear my friends downstairs laughing—the rest of my night is gonna be a lot more fun than sitting here with boring freaking Tammy. I race for my bedroom door and I'm halfway out when I hear her.

"Grace, wait!" she shouts from the computer screen.

"What?" I should have just ended the call.

"Your nightmares, how long have those been happening again? And the gagging? Just since Gloria was kidnapped yesterday? Or longer?" Tammy asks, slipping into an old routine we used to have, back when I used to see her three times a week.

"God Tammy, it's none of your business. You aren't really my therapist anymore, just my dispenser."

She scoffs. "Okay, sorry. Well, if you don't want to tell me about the nightmares, why don't you tell me about school?" she prods.

I can smell hot and spicy pepperoni and ooey-gooey melty cheese. I'm starving! So to placate my former therapist I quickly say, "School is great. I have an amazing boyfriend, Seth, who maybe I'll ask to come over later tonight. I still have the two best friends in the world, Nico and Emma, and they are downstairs waiting for me. Basically my life is perfect Tammy. There. Happy now?"

"Grace, I know it might be hard for you to accept, but we are still family and I enjoy hearing about your life because I... I love you."

I roll my eyes. "Oh please, love? Like that's part of your vocabulary. No Tammy, you used me as your therapy test subject. Family shouldn't use one another for personal gain. But I'm not mad, I'm over it."

"You know that's not accurate." She frowns.

I just want to get out of here. "Look, I'm sorry. I guess I'm just dehydrated and I've been having a lot of migraines, which means more meds."

She nods. Like she could possibly understand what I'm feeling. I bet she's never even taken an OTC pain pill before, let alone this shit she prescribes me. Yeah, I realize she could write herself a script for the "good stuff" if she wanted to. But again, Tammy is a goody-two-shoes with a real Girl Scout image.

"How many more meds?" she inquires.

"Ugh, I don't know, a couple pills a day! But because of the stupid nightmares I haven't been sleeping. One of the side effects of my meds. You should know, you prescribed them, remember?" I fold my arms over my chest.

"Yes, I remember. I am still technically your therapist. Even if you haven't come to a session in a while."

I throw my head back and laugh. "A while? Try like three years!" See, there was an incident at her office and I swore to never see her again, but Mom still took me. Not as often as before, only like every six months, where I would sit in silence. So would Tammy.

Thank God, Nico and Emma come charging in, interrupting this dumb exchange with computer Tammy. I'm sick of her rhetoric. *What?* I know big words.

"Grace! YAY! You're awake. Come on, pizza's here and we saved you the best piece." Nico has sauce on her face.

"And I brought my ring light, I thought we could film that new K-pop dance we've been working on before we get down to business and record our next episode on the podcast," Emma says.

"Wait, which dance?" We work on so many, I never know.

"You know, the one with the arms." Emma throws her arms up, twirls them once and shimmies forward before flipping her hair. Oh yeah, that dance.

I laugh and do the same move. "Yep! I'm ready! Let's go."

Tammy is still up on the screen. God, what's wrong with her? Like doesn't she have anything better to do than watch and eavesdrop on me and my friends? I mean, what does she think, she's going to report back some huge finding to my mom and suddenly I'll need to go back to therapy again?

I can hear Tammy yelling, "Tell your mom to call me! Sorry again about Glor—" as I flick off my bedroom light and shut the door. Fat chance. I don't want to talk to Mom, because I'll just get mad that she called Tammy in the first place. No. What I need now is time alone with my friends. I need to eat pizza and drink Red Bull and listen to our favorite music and record our podcast and laugh all night. I need to push all of these icky feelings and weird dreams deep, deep, deep down.

I sure as shit do NOT want to think about stupid Gloria. God, Tammy! Why'd you have to go and say her name? But there's a nagging memory in my mind, one that seeing Tammy has dredged up. As if I don't have enough to worry about. Now, I can't even control my own mind. As if it's being taken over by some kind of mind-flayer. Ugh. Fine...

Would you like to know what's inside of my brain right now?

Here, you can take a look. I'll be downstairs eating pizza and having fun with my friends. If you see anything interesting, let me know. Because right now, I don't want to give any of this another second of my time:

"Look Leanne, I'm hesitant to officially diagnose Grace with a personality disorder. We know that until *the incident*—well, she was a high-performing and well-adjusted four-year-old. With my help, she has completely suppressed any memories of what happened to her and Gloria. I know it might seem counterproductive, because you want your child to be able to talk about what happened so she can heal. And you think if I provide an official diagnosis, or we use more traditional methods of psychotherapy, that it will give you and Mark some closure. But if we push Grace to go back and relive those memories, she's going to break. My professional opinion is that we terminate our sessions and you just let Grace live her life with her memories fully repressed," Tammy says to Mom in some grand speech.

I'm in the bathroom, pretending to go pee. I know if you stand on the toilet and take off the metal cover to the vent, you can hear what Tammy says in her office.

"No, Tammy, you don't understand..." Mom's voice trails off.

I remember this day! I'm ten years old. My hair is going through that awkward phase and I've got temporary tattoos dotted on my arms. I'm missing a couple teeth and my earlobes throb. Mom took me to get them pierced yesterday at the mall for my birthday. I've been coming to see Tammy for what feels like every day for my entire life. Only this is the first time I've heard her talk to Mom like this. I don't really understand what they are talking about.

What *incident* with me and Gloria? Does she mean those cages and those dogs?

And what does personality disorder mean?

I thought I was coming here to help Tammy, so she could practice working with kids.

When I was little, Mom said her cousin Tammy needed my help. And I felt so proud helping her... I can remember the first time we arrived here like it was yesterday...

Oh God, a memory within a memory! **Wait. I'm not here.** Emma, Nico, and I are done with our pizza and busy going over the script I wrote for the new episode of our podcast. This episode is wild. It's called "The Headlights." I took some old campfire story about an abandoned, rusted car with a tree growing right up the middle of it deep in the Loblolly Pines but added a monster element to it. Yeah, I know. Impressive. And scary too. You really don't want to be alone in the woods when the headlights turn on and a ghost car driven by the devil comes racing through the woods... But enough about my podcast. You're supposed to be in my head, watching a memory (within a memory). Yikes.

Right. I'm four years old.

"Listen Gracey, we're going to go visit my cousin Tammy. You remember her? The one with the black-and-white kitten and the koi pond?" Mommy asks.

"Oooh, yes Mommy! Can I play with the kitten?" I'm sitting in the back seat on my pink booster seat. I think I'm too big for it, but Mommy says I still need it.

"Well, we aren't going to Tammy's house sweetheart, we are going to her new work," Mommy says.

"Ah, why?" I ask. I watch out the window at the clouds. They look so fluffy, like I could reach out and grab them from the sky. I put my hand on the window and hold it there—watching the clouds as they slide through my fingertips.

"Tammy just finished school to become a special friend for kids like you, and I thought maybe you could help her. She needs some practice," Mommy says.

I shrug.

I wonder what Mommy means? Kids like me?

"I'm thirsty, does Tammy have juice?"

"I'm sure she will have snacks and juice and she said she has some brand-new crayons and games for you to play. It will be fun, I promise," Mommy says as her car turns into the driveway of a building that looks like any regular house. "We're here!" Mommy says happily.

I reach for the buckle, because I'm a big girl and I know how to undo it by myself, but something makes me hesitate. The man. The rotten-faced man. Screaming at me not to touch the latch on the cage. Stop trying to escape. He's not going to hurt us, he just likes to watch us play in the yard with the puppies.

I push myself back into my seat and tuck my legs up and hide my face.

"No, Mommy, no, no, no! I don't want to go. Don't leave me, don't make me talk to Tammy. I don't want to go." I am crying. Trembling with unbridled anxiety. My breathing is so fast I see little stars swirling around.

"Oh, sweet Gracey, honey, I'm not leaving you! Listen honey, we are just going to go in for a few minutes and see the new toys and crayons and say hello to Tammy, okay? It's okay, it's okay." Mommy has my car door opened and she leans in and unbuckles me and picks me up. I'm too big to be carried like a baby, but I'm still crying and shaking.

That man from my nightmares.

He seems so real sometimes.

We walk up to the front porch, well Mommy does, and she carries me the entire way. Before she can knock, it opens up and her cousin

Tammy is standing in the doorway, she's pretty. It smells like cookies and I can see inside and it doesn't look scary and I can see a room with a kid-sized table. There's cute stuffed animals and books and rainbow blocks. Everything is new and begging to be played with. I squirm so Mommy will set me down while she talks to Tammy.

Fast forward to my ten-year-old self standing on the toilet eavesdropping.

That was when I learned I was Tammy's real patient.

Watch as I try to put the pieces together. It's a doozy. I got super pissed and even started breaking stuff...

Mom said I was only helping.

Personality disorder?

Psychotherapy?

But what's really driving me up the wall is that this has something to do with GLORIA!

What. The. Hell.

I jump off the toilet seat and don't even flush to keep up the bathroom ruse. Instead, I barge into Tammy's office. I might even kick the door down. I'm not sure, it's kind of a blur.

"What are you two talking about? I heard you!" I shout.

"Grace! Manners!" Mom reminds me.

"I want to know what you mean. I heard you say there was an 'incident' between me and Gloria. She's a brat! She doesn't talk to me. And I'm sick of going to her house on Friday nights, Mom. I have real friends now. I'm ten and I'm old enough to decide who I'm friends with. I don't care that you want us to be friends. I hate her. I hate Gloria!" I shout. Tears are running down my face. "And you know what Dr. Tammy—I hate you too! You lied to me. You and Mom. You said I was your helper. You said I was helping you learn to be a good therapist. You SUCK. YOU SUCK TAMMY!"

I pick up a potted plant from the coffee table and throw it as hard as I can at the wall. The green-and-blue-painted terracotta smashes and the dirt and plant explode all over the floor and wall.

I wait for them to scream at me.

I wait for the anger.

But it doesn't come. Mom and Tammy just look at me.

Finally, Tammy walks over and puts her hand on my shoulder. "Grace, I think it's time that we end this. I appreciate all the help you've given me the last six years. But you're right. I did lie to you. And I'm sorry for that. But, hopefully, in a small way, I have helped you and I want you to remember I will always be here for you—not only as your therapist, but as a part of your family." Then Tammy walks me out of her office and to the front door of the clinic and opens the door. Mom is right behind her and follows us out to the porch.

"I'll call you later Leanne." Tammy gives Mom a hug and then turns around and goes back into her clinic.

"I want to go home." I run to Mom's car.

Chapter Seven

COME OVER PLEASE, I NEED YOU

"Grace, I thought you were done eating! Come on, let's dance!" Emma is setting up her phone on the stand with the ring light.

I quickly finish my last edit note on our podcast script. Then I smile at Emma, right before taking another huge bite of pizza. "But it's soooo good and greasy." I laugh with a mouthful of food. Sauce drips off my lip and lands like a splatter of blood on the paper. "Oops." I stare at the blood—I mean pizza sauce. For a split second I wonder if whoever kidnapped Gloria is feeding her. I thought my energy level was low today; I can only imagine what she must be feeling.

As if reading my thoughts, Nico hands me an energy drink. "Grace, you look like you could use some energy. Come on, the script is great, let's dance for a while."

"Yeah, okay. You're right, sorry." I set down my pizza and crack open the can and start chugging. Mom hates when we stay up all night laughing and dancing and being loud. Well, she says she hates it, but she still lets us do it every weekend and tomorrow she'll wake up and make us a huge pile of pancakes slathered with syrup or pigs in a blanket or her stuffed French toast, the one she saw on that cooking show they film in Savannah. Okay, okay, so *maybeee* I was exaggerating when I said she can't cook. She makes the best breakfast, that apron she always wears isn't just for show.

After a big ol' country breakfast, Mom will offer to drop us off at the Oglethorpe Mall or drive us out to Tybee Island or let us walk up and down River Street while she reads a book on a bench and watches the tourists.

The thought of having a fun weekend with my friends and Mom actually makes me feel *worse*...

Lately I haven't been such a good friend or daughter. I mean, I've spent a lot of Friday nights hanging out with Seth or being alone in my room all weekend. I've felt tired and irritable, like no one understands me. Seth doesn't seem to mind, he plays *Warzone* with his friends online and I lie on his bed with my head in his lap watching *Stranger Things* on my phone and I don't really have to talk or think. But when I'm with Nico or Emma, they expect me to be a certain way. I can't be moody and quiet. Same thing with Mom. If I hide out in my room for more than a few hours she's clucking around like a worried mother hen.

The only person I've told any of it to is Gloria.

Cause, well, like I said, she's a good listener. Shut up about it.

I close my eyes and remember a few weeks ago on our usual morning walk when I was spilling my guts to Gloria, again. "I don't know if you ever feel this way—like sad and tired all the time? Even when you don't know why or don't have anything to be sad about?"

She was doing some stupid walk where she had one foot up on the sidewalk and one foot in the street, so she was bobbing up and down, over and over, up and down instead of our usual fast pace.

"It's like, there's something inside of me trying to escape, trying to break free. I don't know what it is, but it's eating me from the inside, clawing its way out," I said.

Up down, up down.

Her stupid ponytail swinging.

"Like there's this part of me that's missing—but it's on the tip of my tongue, a word I can't quite remember."

But she didn't say a word.

"Oh my God, Gloria! Look at Emma's hair! She dyed it purple!" I screamed and ran towards my friend. Completely forgetting Gloria. Pushing away that gnawing feeling that something in my life was missing, *some part of my life.*

But now, tonight, here with my friends I start feeling it again—

Lonely.

Afraid.

Scared.

Before I know it, it's three a.m. and Emma and Nico are on the couch sleeping, totally crashed from our dancing, singing, and podcast-recording party. I'm sitting in the recliner with my favorite worn-out pillow Mr. Puppy and my phone. I rub the worn velvet of his ears between my fingertips, then gently trace the black stitched X over his left eye. Whoever heard of a one-eyed dog pillow? Doesn't matter, I still love him.

Seth's probably still up playing video games.

I'll call him.

"Seth?" I whisper when I hear him groan.

"Are you okay, Grace?" he mumbles.

"Sorry, I thought you might be awake playing *Call of Duty* or *Valhalla* or something. Go back to sleep," I tell him.

"No, no, I'm up. Do you want me to ride my bike over?" he asks. My heart pounds. Seth really is a good boyfriend. I should be nicer to him. Like, when he wanted to come over tonight—I should have said yes. I mean, I can't pick between him, Nico, and Emma, but I don't have to keep them apart. We can all hang out together.

I guess, I worry he'll think I'm a dork if I'm dancing to K-pop and singing and gossiping and painting nails with my friends. Or he'll get bored and want to leave when we start recording the podcast and blocking trolls on our channel. But maybe I should stop forcing my insecurities on him. I should give him the chance to be part of the group.

"Yeah, come over. But use the alley because those cops are still out front," I whisper. "I'll unlock the back door and you can just come up to my room."

"Can I sleep in your bed with you?" he asks slyly.

"Yes, and we can even snuggle under the covers." I hang up before I change my mind.

I go upstairs and open my parents' room—Dad is snoring loudly. Mom is face down, legs hanging out the side of the sheets. Our old cat Rosco is curled up around her head, chewing on her hair. He glares at me and I flip him off.

"Mom, Seth is coming over and sleeping in my room," I say as softly as I can. This way when Mom opens my door in the morning and sees Seth sleeping in the bed with me, she can't freak out. I'll make sure he crawls back out of the covers before we fall asleep.

"Hmmm?" she says sleepily. "Grace, take Rosco." She bats at the cat with her hand and pulls her legs back into the sheets. Her breathing is heavy, she's already asleep again. I make a face, because I don't want to touch Rosco, but go over and pick him up anyway. He hisses at me and I hiss back at him and then walk out of my parents room and shut the door.

"You're a jerk kitty," I tell Rosco and plop him down on the chair that sits on the landing. He arches his back and yawns at me before curling up to go back to sleep.

I yawn too—three a.m. is a funny time when you've had an energy drink and you're mentally awake, but physically exhausted. The Witching Hour or so it's called; when the veil to this world and the supernatural is at its weakest and all the scary things come out. A dog howls somewhere in the distance outside. I shiver as I walk toward the back door, looking over my shoulder a few times and getting jump scared by some shadows cast by the light from under the microwave, which Mom leaves on every night so no one trips when they walk into the kitchen.

I peer out the window on the back door. No sign of Seth yet. He lives two neighborhoods over. On his bike it should only take ten minutes to get here, especially without cars, because he can ride in the middle of the road. I wait for a few minutes before I go upstairs to my room and turn on the TV and my LED lights. I change into a black tank and my gray sweat shorts and flop down onto my bed and check my phone.

He should be here any minute.

I run my tongue over my teeth. Ew.

I jump up to go brush my teeth. My room has a bathroom attached so I don't even have to go back into the hallway. I should text Seth that Mom's cat is in the chair at the top of the stairs; Rosco likes to attack when you aren't paying attention. Stupid cat.

I quickly brush my teeth to get rid of the metallic tang of leftover energy drink and the film that's formed. I'm sure Seth and I will kiss for a while. My cheeks feel hot thinking about it. Seth is a really good kisser. That's something else we do a lot when we hang out. When he finishes his video games, he'll lean over and kiss me while I'm lying on his lap. And I'll sit up and face him and hold him and he lets me do so for as long as I want. Yeah, I guess he really is the best boyfriend. And he's so smart, smarter than me for sure, but he never makes me feel stupid.

I lie back down on my bed and check my phone. God, where is he? It's already 3:30! I yawn and try calling him. But it goes to voicemail.

I text him.

No response.

I bet he fell back asleep; he did sound tired. I should have known. I wonder if his phone died? YAWN! Well, if he went to sleep, I guess I will too...

Chapter Eight

SETH, WHERE ARE YOU?!

"**G**race." Mom is shaking me awake.

"Whaaaat," I groan. It feels too early to be awake. I look at my phone, I have a ton of missed texts and calls from Seth's mom... That's weird. It's only eight a.m.! What is going on?

"Grace honey, did you say Seth came over last night?" She asks. Her voice is strained and dry.

"Oh, you heard me?" I sit up and rub the sleep from my heavy eyes.

"Did he...Grace, I mean, I don't care—well I do care, but that's a conversation for another time, young lady. I need to know if Seth was here." She's urgent and now I'm worried.

"Am I in trouble?" I ask.

"Grace, Seth's mom called me. Seth left a note that he was coming here last night. She has called his phone, and she tried you, but no one is answering. She's worried because the neighbors found his bike a few blocks from their house. So listen to me—was Seth here last night? Do you know where Seth is?" Mom isn't playing around. There is real panic in her voice and on her face.

My heart is beating *boom, ba-da, boom* like a drum set in my chest. I fly out of bed and run downstairs and out the back door and down the steps and through our yard.

"GRACE!" Mom screams and chases after me.

I'm freaking out.

Oh my God. Where is Seth? Where is my boyfriend?

I go through the back gate into the alley and look up one side and down the other. Maybe he got a flat on his bike and walked the rest of the way. Maybe he got tired and sat down or called one of his friends who drives. Maybe he's here, somewhere. Tears run down my face.

"SETH!" I scream. I keep looking from right to left down the alley. "SETH WHERE ARE YOU?"

"Grace." Mom has reached me and she puts a hand on my shoulder.

I look at her.

She said *he left a note*.

Just like someone else I know who disappeared.

Gloria.

My throat closes up in shock, but my stomach is queasy from energy drinks and pizza and adrenaline. I start gagging. Seth was on his way to me! Oh fuck. Oh no. I fall to my knees. The gravel in the alley splits my skin, but I don't care. Something has happened to Seth, because I told him to come over to my house. Because I was lonely and being needy.

"I told him—" I sob.

"Grace, baby, get up, get up." Mom is crying and begging.

"Seth is gone, Gloria is gone. What's happening, Mom?" I let her pull me up from the ground.

"Mrs. Everly, what's going on? Is everything okay?" It's one of the police officers from the car out front. He's got an old McDonald's bag and he's walking into the alley toward our trash can.

"Get your partner, I think y'all need to come inside with us." Mom wipes her face. "Grace come on, let's get you in and cleaned up. Meet us at the front door if you don't mind, Officer." Mom walks back through the gate and into the house. I know my friends are still sleeping, but I need them.

"I want Nico and Emma," I sob and try to go into the living room.

"No, I'm telling their parents to come get them." Mom takes out her phone and starts texting.

"NO! I don't want them to leave," I cry. Then the doorbell rings. It's the officers, doing like Mom asked and using the front door. I run up to my room and get my phone. Seth's mom has called four more times.

It buzzes again while I'm holding it.

I panic and silence it. What am I supposed to say? *Hi Mrs. Scott, I asked your son to come to my house at three in the morning and now he's missing. And my next-door neighbor Gloria went missing two days ago and the cops are chilling on our block to keep an eye on things. Oh, and I've been having weird dreams about being locked in a cage with Gloria when we were little kids, not to mention I've been blacking out. I'm a real winner. Aren't you so happy your son and I are dating and talking about going to college together someday?*

Yeah, right.

"Seth, where are you?" I open my phone and look at his picture.

I hear everyone downstairs talking so I zip up my black hoodie and slink down the stairs to the kitchen.

"Grace, do you know what happened to Seth?" one of the officers asks me. The other one is on his phone and Mom is texting and pacing around. Dad is standing with a cup of coffee in his hand, but he's not drinking it. He looks like he's seen a ghost and it's really freaking me out.

"Seth was—" I start, but as soon as I open my mouth, Emma is there in the doorway, her faded purple hair matted up and her makeup smeared.

"It's so loud in here! Why are there cops in your kitchen? Did they bring donuts?" She yawns and laughs at her joke.

I start crying and run over and grab her.

"Jesus, Grace, what happened? Did they find Gloria?" Emma's eyes go from tired to fully awake in a split second.

"No. Seth is gone! I told him to come over last night after you and Nico fell asleep, but when he didn't show up, I thought he fell asleep." I wipe my face and I'm a snotty, tear-soaked mess.

"Grace, don't panic, he's probably at Hunter's house or with Cash and the other guys he games with." Emma holds me ferociously. I can feel her breathing, it's uneven. She doesn't even believe her own words.

"They found his bike on the side of the road and he left a note saying he was coming here! But he never made it. I know his mom would have called all his friends." I start crying again.

"What's going on?" Nico walks in and looks around.

"Seth is missing." I choke out the words.

Chapter Nine

DREAMS NIGHTMARES

I can't handle the commotion in the kitchen. More cops show up. Nico and Emma are rushing around calling everyone we know asking if anyone has seen Seth. Emma's mom arrives and starts freaking out. My dad is being weird and Mom is buzzing like she's hosting a dinner party, refilling drinks and offering food. *This is a nightmare.*

"I'm going to take a shower, you guys should go home," I say and hug my friends. "I'll call you later." Emma's mom quickly takes them out the front door as I'm heading upstairs. I don't even want to turn around and watch them walk away. They'll probably never be allowed to come over again. Since the people I love are disappearing.

Ugh. What am I thinking?

I don't love Gloria. She's a troll. A pest. A jerk.

I mean, she was supposed to become my best friend according to our parents, with all our forced Friday night hangouts. It wasn't just the Friday nights. Our moms took us to swim lessons together, and tennis, and ballet. They used to talk about us going to some all-girls college when we were older. I bought into it too, and I really tried all these years. Like maybe it WAS my fault she didn't speak. So I'd speak even more. On our walks, and every time I saw her. Just call me jabber-jaw, because I was always talking.

Then I think about the creepy blackout dreams I had about me and Gloria. The cages, the dogs. I shake them off. Why am I even thinking about her and not about Seth?

I turn on the shower to let it heat up. I stare at my reflection in the mirror.

"You did this," I say to myself. "You told him to come over, you pathetic, needy baby." Steam erases my reflection and I wipe my hand across the mirror to give myself a final glare. Then I turn the music up on my phone and crawl into the shower. The water is hot enough to peel off my skin, but I can barely feel it over the pain in my chest.

I can't believe something happened to Seth. Is there really a kidnapper taking teenagers in Richmond Hill? What are the odds that two people I KNOW have been taken?

I hear Seth's voice in my head. "*Like one in three hundred million.*" The odds that no one saw Gloria. Now, do those same odds apply to his disappearance? I close my eyes and wish I could go back to three a.m. and not call him. Why did I do that? Why did I tell him to come over?

Because I love him.

Because I needed him.

Except there *is a kidnapper.* Someone is stealing my friends. This is what happens on *Stranger Things.* Not in my real life. This is what we spoof about on our podcast. Creepy things that happen in the woods. Like the ghost of Alice Riley, walking around looking for her missing baby. This doesn't actually happen, does it? Yesterday I tried to convince myself that Gloria's disappearance had no effect on me. I grimace. I can't keep lying.

Okay, so maybe I don't know how I feel about Gloria.

Maybe she is my friend and I just didn't realize it. Maybe that's why Mom said we have a friendship (even if she used the words one-sided). Maybe that's why everyone at school thinks we are friends. I try to ignore the noise in my head and pick up the shampoo. But while I wash my hair, a memory floods my mind. Not a dream. No. This is a flashback.

A real memory.

"Do you think you'll ever talk to me again?" I ask as I reach for the brown crayon. Gloria and I are sitting at my kitchen table coloring. Mommy is babysitting. Gloria doesn't answer, but she holds up her picture for me to see. It's us holding hands and running through the tall skinny Loblolly pine trees. There is a one-eyed puppy chasing us. And a dark angry shadow behind the puppy.

"Why did you draw that? It's scary," I say to her. "I don't like to think about the rotten-faced man. Mommy's cousin Dr. Tammy says that I can use my powers to lock out the bad thoughts. See—" I hold up my picture to Gloria. It's me wearing a superhero cape and holding my puppy pillow and Gloria is behind me with a big smile on her face. "See, I use my superpowers to protect you and Mr. Puppy."

"Girls, you ready for some lunch?" Mommy says and comes into the room.

"Yes Mommy, can you make us macaroni and cheese," I say and get up. "Come on Gloria, let's go play Barbies in my room." I put down the crayons and drag Gloria with me. Before we leave, I turn back to Mommy. "Gloria is still upset about the man who took us, Mommy. We need to make her happy so she will talk to me again, maybe she should visit Dr. Tammy with me. She taught me how to block those bad feelings." Then we turn and skip away, hand in hand.

Me and my silent best friend.

The hot water and steam pelt my face.

Waking me from my real memory.

"Oh my God," I whisper.

It's déjà vu. You know that weird feeling you get when you feel like you've been somewhere before, even though you've never been there? Or when you meet someone for the first time, but you swear you've known them your entire life? Yeah, that feeling.

My skin crawls and even the hottest water can't take the chill away from my veins.

My dreams.

They aren't dreams.

They are memories. Horrible and tragic, but very real memories. Gloria and I were kidnapped and locked in a cage like animals by the rotten-faced man. My stomach rolls and lurches and I start vomiting in the shower. I can't stop the pain and fear and horrifying memories as they begin to fill my psyche. One by one. Flashes.

Us in a cage.

The puppies, crying and barking.

"Grace." Mom is knocking on the door. But I don't answer.

The rotten-faced man.

"Grace..." Frantic knocking.

Me and Gloria. Locked in a cage.

"Grace, honey, please, are you okay?" she pleads.

I'm sitting on the floor of my shower.

The water is ice cold now. I can't feel a thing.

I'm numb. I'm a girl in a cage.

And now—Gloria and Seth are gone and I know who has them. It has to be him. That's why Gloria left that note. To lift my veil. To force me to remember.

Ask Grace.

Chapter Ten

Dad Tries To Help (But Kind of Makes It Worse)

"Look what fucking happened when we let medical professionals help us last time, Leanne—" Dad spits the words at Mom.

"Don't blame Tammy for this, Mark. She did the best she could!" Mom snaps with just as much venom.

"We should have taken Grace and moved as far away from this town as possible. But we stayed. Why did we stay? Huh? Remind me again? Oh riiiiighht... Your friends, your tennis club, your—"

"Just shut the fuck up Mark, you're the one with the big-time gym and all your stupid clients you didn't want to leave." Mom reaches over like she's going to slap Dad in the face.

"Stop," I moan. "Get out of my room." I'm on my bed and I pull the blankets over me. I'm shaking. I'm wet and cold. And the last thing I want to do is listen to my perfect parents have an argument over how they failed me and all their pathetic problems. Mom and Dad busted through the lock of my bathroom and pulled me out of the shower, cold, naked, and babbling like an idiot. Mom wanted to take me to the emergency room. Dad told her no way, we would handle this ourselves.

Yeah, they are really handling it.

"Grace, honey, I'm so sorry!" Mom redirects. "Please, please, you have to understand." She's tender and loving and all that hate in her voice has evaporated.

"Grace, baby girl." Dad sits on my bed and pets my wet head.

Like a dog.

My eyes roll up into my head as a migraine slams into me and then everything goes black.

***

"...Come 'ere lil pups... you want your dinner?" His voice is raspy and croaky. Like a frog. My mouth gets wet when I hear his voice. Because I'm starving.

"Don't do it," Gloria whispers.

I can't help it. I crawl over to the edge of the cage and whimper.

"Good girl, thas'a nice lil pups," he says and reaches into the cage, but I back up with fear when I see his square shaped fingers. Slowly and carefully, I sniff the air around his hands. It's peanut butter and jelly! I practically pee myself with excitement.

His fat fingers are covered in a thick slabs of brown, creamy goo—the kind Mommy buys. The Jiff creamy cause I hate the chunky kind. And that's grape jelly, the one in the purple jar that's runny and super sweet. I know if I crawl just a little closer, I can lick it off the man's fingers.

Drool is dripping out the sides of my mouth and my stomach and throat cramp up.

Food.

I need it so badly I can't think.

Then there is a sharp pain in the back of my calf. I turn around to tell Gloria not to pinch me. She can have her turn next! And I see her, she's not pinching me. She's biting me! She's biting me hard and I cry out in pain, "OUCH! Stop it Gloria!"

The man jerks his hand back automatically and slams his fist into the wall behind him. The peanut butter and jelly splatters across the paint. My stomach protests at the waste. The man is angry, very angry. He starts to yell and kicks the cage. "Little bitches! Mind your manners!"

Gloria and I yelp out from the sudden jolt.

I think the man likes our yelping—because he starts laughing and kicks the cage again, harder this time. "That's right, filthy little bitches." The other dogs yip and howl and cry and whine.

I think they are sad for us.

Gloria grabs ahold of me tight as she can to keep us steady through his abuse.

"Sorry," I cry into her shoulder.

"Remember, you are brave." She holds me tight.

***

I sit up straight in bed.

It wasn't a nightmare. It was real. Gloria and I were locked in a cage together, like dogs. Until we escaped. And now the rotten-faced man has Gloria and Seth.

I know it with every ounce of my being.

"I'm awake. And I'm really sick of blacking out."

"How much do you remember?" Dad asks. His voice is weepy. I don't blame him... But I'm still bitter and I turn my back to him. "Do you want to talk about it?" he adds softly.

"Yeah, I guess."

"Then let's get out of here. Get dressed and meet me downstairs in ten minutes."

Now, we're sitting on a big plaid blanket out on the white sands of Tybee Island and the sun is making the water shimmer and dance in patterns. As soon as Dad turned towards Savannah, I knew where he was taking me. To the beach. My favorite place in the world. I didn't argue, even though I had no desire to come here. I just want to be home, in my bed, crying and waiting to see if Seth calls.

It feels like we sit and stare at the water for hours, long enough to watch a giant cargo ship full of red and blue and green containers stacked five-high slowly crawl out of the mouth of the Savannah River and onto the open ocean. My breathing quickens and my head spins—what if Seth is trapped in one of those containers? I can't stop staring at the ship, bile rising, and even the beauty of the egrets and herons swooping down to catch fish can't stop my mind from imagining the worst.

It's really a shame too, because if I wasn't drowning inside of my head, I'd say how beautiful it is. I'd take pictures or make a stupid video and send it to Seth.

Seth.

He's gone.

I gasp for breath and put my hands up to my throat and try not to choke.

"Dad," I moan.

"Grace, oh sweetie." Dad bursts into tears and inches closer to me but I flinch and wrap my arms around my knees and focus on the constant rhythm of the waves.

Just breathe, I remind myself.

The sound of the waves lapping on the shore and the wind blowing salt spray in my face is just enough to keep me from going totally catatonic.

"Did those things that I remember really happen to me?" I finally have the nerve to ask Dad, who is a complete crying mess, which feels so wrong because he's such a big, muscled dude.

There's a young couple walking by on the beach in front of us and they seem concerned, like they want to stop and ask if I'm okay. I shoot them a nasty look and they keep walking. But something inside me snaps.

"YEAH KEEP WALKING ASSHOLES!" I scream at the couple, even though they are way down the beach by now. They don't even turn around to look at me.

"Grace." Dad straightens up and wipes his face.

I can't stop. It feels good to scream! So I stand up and shake the sand off me and point at Dad. "No Dad," I yell. "FUCK YOU!" I scream. It's exhilarating. So, I throw my head back and start screaming. "AAAaaahhhhh!"

Seriously, what's wrong with me?

Are you watching this? I'm clearly out of control.

"Grace," Dad says. He gets up and stands next to me. He's not shushing me or telling me to be quiet. He's just standing there, trembling.

My blood is hot, I can feel it coursing through my body, pumping like the beat of a heavy metal song. Tears stream down my cheeks. I slap myself across the face.

"Grace!" Dad puts his hands up to stop me. But Dad can't protect me from myself.

Just like he didn't protect me from him.

"Don't you understand? My entire life is a lie. My dreams, these fucked-up things in my head—" I pound the side of my head with my fist. "They're real. That man, with the rotten face. He's real. Me and Gloria being locked in a dog cage. That was real. Seth and Gloria getting kidnapped. That's real." My teeth are clenched and I'm basically just whisper-screaming with my lips.

Dad flinches.

I can't stand seeing him like this or listening to myself berate him. So I turn and run in a sprint straight toward the water. I don't care that I'm wearing sweatpants and a hoodie. I don't care that I'm not a great swimmer. Something in me has broken and I have to get as far away from here as possible. I dive into the warm blue Atlantic and start paddling.

"GRAAACE!" Dad bellows. The sound is so far off and distant. I close my eyes and swim as hard and as fast as I can.

One, two, three, four, push, push, breathe, go Grace, go Grace...

I'm in a trance.

The waves and the saltwater cocoon me and the current helps pull me further and further into the ocean. I rip my hoodie off and let it drift down without missing a stroke.

Keep going. Keep pushing.

***

"Come on Gloria," I pant. "We have to keep going before the man catches us." I am pulling on my friend, running through the woods.

Pine needles stab my feet, but I don't care, we can't stop. We have to keep going. Keep pushing.

The little one-eyed puppy barks. Urging us to run faster.

I got the keys. I unlocked our cage, but I couldn't leave the one-eyed puppy. She woke up and cried for me. And I'm brave, Mommy says I'm strong and I can do anything I want, especially if I'm a good girl and I work hard and do my best. *I want to save Gloria and the little one-eyed puppy.*

"Graaaace, I'm tired and my feet hurt," Gloria complains and tries to let go of my hand.

"Don't let go," I say and pull Gloria into the thick underbrush of the saw palmettos. It is snagging and tugging on us, trying to keep us from escaping.

"PUPS!" the rotten-face man screams in the distance. "I'LL FIND YOU! YOU CAN'T HIDE FROM ME!"

One-eyed puppy whimpers and lies on the ground.

"Come on puppy, we have to go." I urge her to follow us. But she's frozen and Gloria starts to cry.

I want to cry too. I want my mommy. I close my eyes and imagine Mommy. She's in the pool and I'm on the edge. "Grace, come on baby. Just jump in and swim. One, two, three, breathe. You can do it. You can do anything."

"We can do anything." I squeeze Gloria's hand as hard as I can and pull her out of the mess of thorns and branches, getting us into a clearing where we can run again. I move as fast as I possibly can.

We can't wait for little puppy to follow us and my eyes are blurry with tears. I want her to come home with me, but I want my mommy even more. I want Gloria to get home to her mommy. I just want to get away from here. We are faster than the rotten-faced man. He has a hurt leg. He can't run fast. But we can run fast. One, two, three, push harder, faster, keep going, keep going, don't stop, just breathe.

But finally I stop.

I'm not running in the woods with Gloria.

I'm in the ocean, out as far as I could possibly be. My sweatpants are long gone, pulled off by their bloated water weight. The sun has set and it's dark. I look around and I can't see the shore. I can't see my dad or hear him calling for me.

Maybe I'm underwater.

I don't know, so I roll over and kick into a back float and look up into the sky and search for the faint glow of the early evening stars. Then I kick my legs and flip back on my stomach. And there, to my left, I see tiny twinkling lights in the windows of the houses on the beach. They are so far they're barely visible. I could swim back if I really wanted to. Or I could just let the ocean consume me. My heart is clenched up inside of my chest. There's too much happening for me to make a decision. Live or die, I don't really care.

And then, out of nowhere, I hear Gloria's voice.

"Ask Grace."

Fuck you, Gloria. You made me remember. You did this. I exhale and let myself drift down under the waves.

Chapter Eleven

SOMETIMES YOU GOTTA PUNCH IT OUT

"Grace, I think your father and I owe you an explanation," Mom says as she puts a plate of golden pancakes in front of me at the kitchen table. I'm sure they smell good, slathered in rich butter and real maple syrup, but I hardly notice. My head is pounding and my heart is aching. All I want to do is go back to bed and sleep until this entire shit show is over.

Dad, being the hero, swam out and dragged me back to shore last night, just as I was about to succumb to a watery grave. Then he wrapped me up in our sandy plaid beach blanket and put me in the backseat of the car and drove me home.

He looked like a mad man. Saltwater dripping from his hair, glasses steamed up, hands white-knuckling the steering wheel. He ignored Mom's sobs when she saw us after we finally pulled into the driveway. I ignored her too and ran up to my room and slammed the door hard enough to shake the windows and knock off all our family photos.

Mom pushes the pancakes a little closer to me and scoots the fork over with her pointer finger.

"Oh really? You think you owe me an explanation?" I pick up the cutlery and stab it into the middle of the stack of pancakes, like it's a creature with tentacles about to attack me. "I'm not hungry." I shove the plate to the middle of the table, a trail of syrup sliding behind it.

"Fair enough." Mom nods.

"Damn it, Grace, this is hard for us too." Dad stands so fast his chair tips over. He takes one step forward, as if he's going to pace—"No, Mark, sit down. We discussed how this was supposed to go," Mom demands. But Dad stays vertical.

"How *this* is supposed to go? Like, you've known there are things you've kept secret from me, and you've rehearsed how to tell me?" My knees are wobbly, but I stand anyway. If Dad doesn't have to sit, neither do I.

"Now, hold on a gosh darn second. Both of you sit DOWN." Mom slams her hands on the table and rattles the bottle of syrup. It startles me. When I look at her face, there is a fire in her eyes, a look I don't see often. I let out a long-exacerbated sigh.

"Fine." I slump in my chair.

Dad growls and sits.

"Grace, there's no point in beating around the bush here. You might be in serious danger. We have to tell you what we know, about what happened to you and Gloria. You have to listen to me and understand that—" Mom's voice is shaking. She's trying to be firm so I'll get her point. But she just sounds angry and pissed off, and I really don't appreciate it. I'm the one who's going through all this shit. Not her. The least she could do is show me a little compassion!

"I get it, Mom. Me and Gloria were kidnapped when we were little kids. I remember bits and pieces of it. But somehow we escaped. Is that what you are trying to tell me?" I finish what I think she was trying to tell me, because if I say it, rather than hear someone else tell me, then *I have the control*. I can make it sound as if I'm not crushed by the reality of it. I can make my parents think I'm okay.

But I'm not okay. Some weirdo freak locked us in a cage next to a bunch of dogs. How can anyone be *fine* after something like that? The more I remember about what happened to me and Gloria, the more I realize nothing was ever really what it seemed. I've been living in some upside-down world. It's my house, my life, but there is a darkness over everything. I look around the room; sunlight might be streaming through the delicate white lace curtains over the kitchen sink, but it's muted by this revelation.

"I don't think you understand," Mom says softly.

"I do!"

But clearly Mom's not content to let me think I know everything, with how her eyes dart back and forth from me to Dad.

"Jesus! Stop looking at us like that!" I snap at her.

She purses her lips, bows her head and closes her eyes. "Grace, I need you to listen to me. I need you to take a deep breath and just hear me out."

Oh great, so there *is* more.

"If you want the police to find Gloria and Seth, you're going to have to dig deep, baby girl. I know you are starting to remember bits and pieces. We are going to help you rip that Band-Aid off. Because maybe you'll be able to remember something new or you can explain it better than when you were four." Mom opens her eyes and reaches for the pancakes that are still sitting in the middle of the table. She takes out the fork and stabs it a few times. "That's sort of satisfying, isn't it?" A smile slides across her face.

I can't help but smile too.

"Yeah, let me do it again," I say and reach out toward the fork and plate. I take it from Mom and jab the pancake monster over and over.

Dad chuckles. Then his eyes brighten as if a lightbulb goes off in his head. "Hold on. Stop murdering the pancakes, I have a much better idea." He stands up and jogs out of the kitchen. I hear his keys jingle from the bowl on the table next to the front door. "Well, aren't you coming?" he shouts. Mom and I both jump and race to the front entry. Dad's got the door open.

"I'm not dressed to go anywhere!" I complain. I'm in pajama shorts and an oversized T-shirt. My hair is sloppy and I don't have any make-up on. Mom looks about like I do. Our Sunday clothes. Meant for lazy mornings and cleaning house or doing yard work. Not for hitting the town.

"You both look perfect." Dad smiles and waves us along with him. So, without too much of a fight, we follow and load up in the Range Rover and Dad turns on music and starts singing as loud as he can and rolls the windows down. This isn't really his style. But Mom and I keep going with it and start singing along.

It feels good to forget that I'm living in a strange and alternate world where Gloria and Seth are gone, even if it's only because I'm in temporary shock from the sudden rush out of the house and loud music. I roll down the window and put my arm out, waving it up and down in the humid southern wind as Dad drives out of our neighborhood and turns on Main Street.

"What are we doing at your work?" I ask when Dad turns into the parking lot behind the refinished two-story brick building.

"A little physical therapy."

"What the hell does that mean?"

"Grace," Mom scolds.

"I mean, what the *heck* does that mean?" I roll my eyes.

"It means you're gonna punch this shit out of your system—not stab a plate of pancakes," Dad says. Mom smacks his arm for cursing.

"Yeah, well, maybe I like stabbing pancakes."

Dad snorts. "This is what we should have done all along. Not dance class and tennis lessons. Or play dates at Tammy's house."

Mom makes a sound like a cross between an angry cat and a pig grunt and jumps out of the vehicle before Dad's even turned it off. She slams the door and marches across the parking lot and into the employee entrance.

"Jeez, what's got her all bent out of shape?" I ask.

"Me. She doesn't like me interfering like that. She truly believed that all the lessons and seeing her cousin every week for therapy would fix you."

"Oh, I didn't realize I was broken."

"Dammit, Grace! You've had a serious trauma. We've got to do something to get it out of you, to flush your system—"

"But Daaaaad," I whine as I drag myself out of the Rover and cross my arms. I stand in the parking lot dreading going inside the building. It's not one of those cutesy gyms where teenage girls go to dance and do yoga. This gym is for tough guys. Guys like my dad. You know, like boxing, weightlifting, that kind of super macho crap. He always begs for me to come and train, but um, excuse me, gross and sweaty.

Dad doesn't tolerate my moaning and groaning, and heads for the back door. I follow him inside. It's dark in the back hallway, there's heavy metal music coming from beyond the wall, and when the door closes behind me, my heart races, I feel trapped and like a thousand dark eyes are watching me.

"Dad, where'd you go?" I spin around disoriented.

"This way, Grace." Dad's voice echoes. His feet pounding up the metal staircase from the end of the hall. I race up behind him, not wanting to be left alone in the dark. It's been forever since I've come to the gym with him.

He flips a switch and the white overhead lights are jarring; I cover my face, the clash of dark and light feels painful somehow. At the top of the stairs, he unlocks his office and I step inside. There is a huge glass window that overlooks the gym floor. I'm surprised by how much activity is going on down there. There's a boxing ring with people sparring. Along the wall is a row of punching bags. There's a rope that goes up to the ceiling and people taking turns pulling themselves up. And all kinds of heavy weight machine equipment. On the far side is a huge new MMA cage and a big crowd of people watching some training exercises.

"Wow, I forgot what it was like on the floor. Did you expand over there, Dad? That MMA cage is new." I put my hand on the glass.

"Yeah, I bought out Mr. Kirkpatrick's shop when he retired a few years ago. We just finished the renovations and opened up the new cage and there's a big room behind it for classes. I hired two new trainers and next month we're even starting a youth program. My goal is to make this thing more than just a place for *Meat Heads*, as your mother so lovingly calls us," Dad says.

I look over my shoulder and see Mom standing in the doorway. She walks up and puts her arms around him. "Sorry babe, I hope you know how proud of you I am," she says and gives him a big kiss.

"Gross. I thought this was about me getting out my anger, not about you two getting sappy and romantic," I sneer, spotting my old boxing gloves on a hook on the wall near Dad's desk. While my parents keep kissing, ignoring me, I snatch the gloves off the wall. I try to tug one over my hand and realize it's waaaaay too small. "Dad."

They are really going at it. "MOOOM, DAAAAD!"

"Hmmm... oh, Grace, sorry." Dad coughs. Mom looks sheepish.

"My gloves don't fit me anymore. How am I supposed to punch out my anger if I don't have gloves that fit?" I hand him the gloves and cross my arms.

"Let's go down to the shop and have Max fit you for a new pair. I think you might know Max. He goes to your school—good kid. I hired him a few months ago, he works in the shop on the weekends," Dad explains as we go out the door and down the front set of stairs that lead out onto the main floor of the gym.

"Max works here? You never told me that." I frown. Max. There's only one Max at school and that's Max Fischer. He's the guy Gloria talks to outside of study hall. I see the way she smiles and bats her eyes at him. She's totally in love. Not that she'd tell me about it. My face starts to heat up thinking about Gloria.

Everything comes back to me, like a salty ocean wave slapping me in the face.

Gloria.

Seth.

"Grace, are you okay?" Mom turns around and asks when she realizes I've stopped in my tracks. She puts her hand out to steady me.

"Yeah, I'm just feeling shitty, about Seth and Gloria." I pause. I don't know what else to say.

"Your dad's right, let's get you some gloves and go hit the punching bag a few times." Mom guides me the rest of the way to the shop.

You can buy boxing gloves and tape and shirts with the gym logo on them. There's protein powders and vitamins and water bottles and towels too. From the looks of it, Dad must have expanded the shop during his remodel. There's more swag here than I remember. I see Max behind the counter. He's watching a video that's playing on the TV that hangs behind the desk. The MMA movie *Warrior*. I know it because it's Dad's favorite; he cries every time he watches it, which is like all the time.

"Hey boss, we've had a big morning. I sold two pairs of gloves and a membership," Max says when he sees Dad. He's wearing a shirt with the gym logo on the front. "Oh, hey, Grace." He sobers and drops his gaze when he notices me. His sandy hair falls over his face and he does that head shake to swoop it over.

"Max," I mumble back.

"Great job, Max." Dad pats him on the back when he goes behind the counter to look at the computer screen.

"Yeah, and there have been a ton of calls about the new kids and teen classes. I think word is getting out about Glo—" But he doesn't finish saying her name. "Parents want their kids to learn self-defense." The phone rings, interrupting Max. He picks it up and I can tell it's another parent wanting their kid in classes. He starts asking questions and writing information down on a clipboard.

"Mark, we should have thought of this a long time ago," Mom whispers to Dad.

"Well, better late than never." Dad rubs his face. He heaves a heavy long sigh before walking over to the display of Hayabusa boxing gloves and grabs a pair. He hands them to me. "Try these ones on for size, kiddo."

I take the navy-blue gloves from him and tug one of them on. It fits like a glove, as they say. "Mom, can you help me get the other one on?" She tugs it over my right hand, then laces them both on tight. They feel good. It's been so long since I've donned a pair of boxing gloves. I'm not sure I remember how to do the punches like Dad once taught me. But the adrenaline is already starting to fill me up and I roll my shoulders and tilt my head side to side.

Max smiles when he sees me. "So, Grace, you gonna start working out here? I was surprised when your dad said you hardly ever come by. Man, if my dad owned a gym like this, I'd be here every day." I can tell he means well, but it just makes me feel guilty and bad about myself. Then I see it, a look in his eyes. He's going to ask me about Gloria. I tense up. Because I don't want to talk about her with him.

Ring! Ring!

Saved by the phone. I smile and shrug as Max answers the phone and starts taking down more information on the clipboard again.

"All right, you've got gloves, and here's a mouthguard." Dad shoves a piece of plastic rubber in my mouth. "Let's go hit some bags."

I walk out of the shop and head for the main gym floor. It smells like sweat, dirty socks, and testosterone. I wrinkle my nose for a second until I get used to it. The floor is broken out into different sections and seems a lot bigger down here than when I was standing in Dad's office looking out the window. There are three huge guys lifting weights and grunting. A couple guys my age are climbing the rope to the ceiling. Some big dudes are in the boxing ring throwing punches and being shouted at and coached by their entourages.

It's overwhelming.

I had no idea the gym was this packed.

"Is it like this every day?" I ask with a lisp from the mouthguard. Dad nods as we make our way to the long row of punching bags. Most are taken, by guys grunting and groaning, and slugging the black bags as hard as they can. We find an open one near the end of the row and Dad stands behind it to steady it for me to hit.

"I want you to come here after school from now on. Mom can drive you or you can ride the bus here," he says. "Now punch the bag, Grace."

"What?" I exclaim. "I'm not coming here after school. I walk home with Gloria every day." Tears well up in my eyes and I look around nervously realizing my mistake. I used to walk home with Gloria every day. I don't walk home with her anymore because she's missing. Someone has kidnapped her. Just like they did when we were little.

A fire builds up inside my gut.

A burning flame.

A ball of fiery anger, and before I know what I'm doing, I'm punching the bag. It feels good to let out the pain and frustration that has been building up inside of me. I punch with my left arm, then my right, then left, right, again and again, harder and harder.

"Good girl. Let it out," Mom says. "Much better than a fork and a plate of pancakes."

"Hit it, Grace. And then tell me about the man who took you and Gloria from the park when you were four." Dad's voice is strong and demanding.

Something about that question.

It triggers a memory.

There's a pain behind my left eye, like I'm going to get a migraine and I moan and wince. "Daaaaad. I'm getting a migraine," I whine.

"Goddammit, Grace. Fight against the pain. Hit the bag again and tell me about the man. Fight it, Grace," Dad urges me.

I pull my arm back and then lean in and give it everything I've got and punch the bag with all my might, to knock out the pain inside my brain, to knock out the pain in my heart. To knock loose the memories of what happened to me as a child.

Not just me.

Me and Gloria.

Chapter Twelve

HAVEN'T YOU HEARD?

"Look, Gloria, puppies!" Four-year-old me runs toward the two puppies playing in the bushes at the far edge of the playground.

"Wait for me Grace," Gloria yells. I'm not waiting for her. She's slow. I run fast because I go to soccer practice and Mommy says I'm a super racer. I put my arms out like I'm an airplane and start running with all my might.

"Y'all don't go too far!" I hear Mommy yell after us. I look back over my shoulder. Mommy and Gloria's mommy are on the bench talking and laughing. I love when Mommy laughs. She's the best mommy in the entire universe!

Gloria is running next to me now, with her arms out like a plane too. We make zooming sounds all the way to the bushes where I saw the puppies.

"Come here little puppies," I call. "Hmmm... I wonder where they went?" I try to snap my fingers, and Gloria giggles.

"No, Grace, like this." She tries to snap, but it sounds worse than mine.

"Yip! Rrrrrrruff!" A little brown and white puppy darts out in front of me and chases after a blue ball.

"Wait for me puppy!" I yell and follow the puppy down the hill and into the big grassy part of the park beyond the playground area. This is where they had the Easter egg hunt a few weeks ago. Me and Gloria found the golden egg with the super ticket we traded for a big chocolate bunny! "Look, Gloria, that's where we found the golden egg." I am running hard after the puppy; I only slow a little when I look over my shoulder and smile at Gloria.

"Watch out!" she screams. But it's too late. I run right into something and it all happens so fast; it's not a wall or a tree, no, it's a person. A man.

He laughs. "Whoa, slow down." He wraps his big arms around me in a hug. But it's too hard and I writhe to get out of his grip.

He keeps laughing and I open my mouth to scream for my mommy, but he covers it. I don't know what to do, and neither does Gloria, because she's frozen in place. Her big brown eyes are filled with tears. I feel a bee sting me in the neck and the man takes his hand off my mouth.

"Mommy," I squeak.

Then the world goes dark.

***

"He stuck me with a needle!" I scream and punch the bag. "I remember! I remember! We were at the park chasing after a puppy and the man, he grabbed me and I thought I got stung by a bee—but it must have been a needle!" I punch the bag again. I'm panting and out of breath. And my migraine isn't a migraine after all. Now that the memory came back to me, the pain in my head evaporated.

"That bastard!" I shriek and punch the bag again, before stopping and putting my gloved hands on my hips. I walk around a little, sucking air in my nose and out my mouth, then I lean up against the punching bag. Mom puts her hands on my shoulders and rubs, keeping my muscles from cramping up.

"Grace, maybe this is enough of a memory for now. I think we should stop." She keeps rubbing, using her thumbs to get that spot where the blade and muscle meet. It feels good and I roll my neck and head from side to side.

"Your mom's right. Maybe this is enough for today," Dad says and steps away from his position as my punching bag spotter.

"No, I have to know what happened to us. Like, how long were we gone? Where did he take us? I need answers!" I shrug Mom off and go back to punching the bag. Without Dad holding it, it moves around wildly.

"Grace, be careful. Watch your form. Don't be erratic or you'll hurt yourself."

"I want answers!" I scream. Dad looks around nervously. I'm sure he's worried I'll freak out all his customers. I mean, if I was them, I'm not sure I'd want to do my workout around some crazy teenage girl beating the living shit out of a punching bag. My adrenaline is starting to wane, and maybe Dad is right. Maybe I should stop before I hurt myself.

Then something interesting starts to happen; the music lowers, and all the guys working out slow their pace, stepping away from their sparring and weights, quietly coming to form a circle around me.

I punch the bag again. "I want some answers! Who did this to me? Tell me his name!" Punch, kick, elbow. Faster. I'm breathing heavy.

"Get it," someone says.

"Left hook!"

"Upper cut!"

The guys are cheering and whistling every time I connect a punch. Their admiration is fueling me. Beads of sweat fly from my brow, I'm on fire and there is no stopping me. My body is alive and ready to unlock years of suppressed memories. I laugh a little when I realize they've been trying to escape. As migraines. As outbursts directed at my mom. As bitter and tart energy toward Gloria.

"I want fucking answers!" I shout and hit the bag. Dad frowns at my language, but it makes all the guys cheer even louder.

"Yeah Mark, she wants fucking answers!" yells some huge guy.

"Tell me! Tell me about the prick who kidnapped me and locked me in a cage!" I'm finally out of steam and stop punching. I suck in air in big gulps and gasps. I wipe my brow. Which isn't that easy to do when you have boxing gloves tied on your hands. I spit on the floor. My arms feel like Jello and my legs are so weak I can hardly stand. "Dad, I need to know." I sink to my knees.

"We don't know baby girl." Dad crouches down next to me.

"Grace, are you okay?" It's Max. Ugh, that's kind of embarrassing. Was he watching this whole time?

"No, not really," I moan.

"What happened?" he asks and reaches out a hand to help me to my feet.

The music is loud again, and almost everyone scatters back to their workouts. A few linger, hoping to know more about whatever is going on with me.

"Haven't you heard? My parents had me in some kind of memory suppression bullshit my entire life. And now all I want to do is remember so I can find Gloria and Seth..." I say as I start to unlace my gloves with my teeth.

Dad reaches for my gloved hand. "Let me do it."

"No." I snatch my hand away from him, and Mom flinches.

"I don't understand, what does that mean? What memories were you suppressing and why would that help you find Gloria and Seth?" Max asks.

Oh, so maybe he wasn't watching the whole time.

"Max, I guess there's no hiding it. Grace and Gloria were kidnapped when they were four years old," Mom admits. "They were missing for about two weeks."

"What? Holy shit, that's wild," he says and rubs his hands over his face as he tries to process the information.

"Yeah, well what's worse is that Mom put me in repressive therapy to make me forget what happened. But it might be helpful to remember, because I think whoever kidnapped us back then is the same person who took Gloria and Seth now."

"Whoa." Max looks at my mom and then at my dad. "Don't you know what happened to them? Can't you just tell her so her memories will come back?"

Mom shakes her head. "The police found Grace and Gloria wandering on Swamp Road at the edge of the Okefenokee Nature Preserve over a hundred miles from here. There's not a person or house anywhere near there. The police said the kidnapper must have dumped them there, but you girls insisted you'd run away."

"So, the cops never found the kidnapper?" Max asks.

Mom shakes her head.

Dad scowls and crosses his arms. The vein in his neck is bulging.

"If the cops couldn't find the kidnapper, maybe you guys should have tried harder," I mumble.

I mean, if it was me, and someone kidnapped my child—I wouldn't sleep until the asshole was found and put in jail. Right? What would you do if someone kidnapped the person you loved most in the world?

"Grace, it wasn't that easy." Mom tries to justify why they didn't hunt him down themselves. "I was just so happy to have you home in one piece! You girls were smelly and hungry and tired, but you weren't hurt. The hospital did a full evaluation, and said you were okay."

"Yeah. If we were so *A-OK* then why did you want to repress my memories?"

"Grace, don't," says Dad. "You don't have any idea what it was like for us when you came home. You cried all the time, and then Gloria stopped speaking to you, and it was a big nightmare. We just wanted you to go back to the happy little girl you were before the kidnapping."

"I thought you were mad that Mom had me working with Tammy."

"I am, I mean, I guess I wasn't back then—" He pauses. "I don't know."

"Oh, you don't know? I can't believe you and Mom. You didn't try to hunt down the guy and kill him, you didn't want to hear me crying so you put me in repressive therapy, and you've spent my entire life lying to me, letting me think I'd done something wrong and that's why Gloria didn't speak to me. And now Gloria and Seth are missing!"

I shake my head.

Max wraps his arms around me and gives me a big hug and whispers, "I'm sorry for what happened to you and Gloria." Finally, someone shows me some freaking compassion. I'm angry at my parents in an entirely new way and I'm glad to have Max here as a witness. I let my shoulders sag and I rest my head on him, sniffling a few times as tears bubble up and pour out of my eyes.

After crying on Max for a few minutes I take a step back. "I'm tired. I want to go home."

Chapter Thirteen

I'M DEAD ON THE INSIDE

Days go by. I stay in bed and I don't answer my phone.

Nico and Emma come to see me and Mom tells them I'm not feeling well.

Dad comes to my room and I ignore him.

Mom cries at night—loud enough for me to hear.

I don't care.

Seth is gone.

Gloria is missing.

I'm dead on the inside.

Chapter Fourteen

With a Little Help From My Friends

"Grace, Max is here to see you," Mom says and opens my door without knocking. She is so annoying. "He said he'll wait, if you want to get cleaned up before you come down."

"Fuck off," I say and pull the blankets up tighter around my body and up over my head. What? I'm mad at my mom. Plus, I've hardly eaten in so long that my stomach is contracted and I think I might really be dying. I'm cold, I'm tired, I'm in pain.

"I will not fuck off, young lady!" Mom walks over and flings open my curtains. The light makes my blanket glow... I know my eyes will scream when I take the blankets off my face. "Get up. You've spent enough time moping in your room. You can't ignore your friends forever."

I groan and hiss when I peel back the covers. Mom is standing at the foot of my bed with her hands on her hips. She looks like a fake person with a floral apron tied around her waist over one of her nice dresses.

"Why are you all dressed up?" I ask her. I climb out of my bed too quickly and my head swoons. I have to put my arms out for balance.

"I'll tell you if you get cleaned up and come downstairs," she says and shuts the door. Oh great. Not only is Max downstairs waiting for me, but Mom is totally up to something weird. My stomach lurches. Maybe Mom is right—I have been in bed for so long, I'm pretty sure there is a permanent butt print where I've sunk into the mattress. So, I take the "Max Bait" and trudge into the bathroom to shower the bed grime off me. I spend way too long in the hot water hoping it will burn away my memories of what happened to me and Gloria.

And Seth.

I miss Seth.

Just as I'm done getting dressed and jump scare myself when I see the time on the clock, there's a soft knock on my door.

"Grace?" Max says through the wood. "I have to get to work, your mom said I could come up to see if you're ready yet, because, I uh... I want to ask you something."

Wait, what? What on earth could Max possibly want to ask me? This is kind of weird right? I mean, you don't think he's here to ask me out, is he? Because that would be totally crossing a line.

Knock, knock. "Grace?"

"What is it, Max?" I throw open my door.

"Oh hey." His face blooms with a deep shade of pink. "Um, do you want to come hang out with me at the gym today? You know, we could watch movies and sell gloves and check membership cards." He laughs nervously.

I narrow my eyes.

He rubs the back of his neck before shoving his hands in his pockets.

"Why are you being so nice to me?" I blurt out.

"Oh, um. I mean, after the last time I saw you, I figured you could use a friend."

Now it's my turn to blush. "Sure, yeah, thank you. That sounds good," I reply. "But I need to eat something. Can we get waffles on the way?" I grab my phone and sweatshirt and you know, it actually feels good to be moving and to have someplace to go.

"Uh yeah, that was easier than I expected," he jokes. "I thought maybe you'd kick and punch me like that bag at the gym."

"Really?" I laugh. "Why would I do that?"

"Because." He looks over my shoulder at my room. "I can tell you haven't left your room in days."

"Oh, shut up." I smack his arm.

I don't even say goodbye to Mom. I want to get the hell away from her. They say there are stages to grief, and that's what I'm going through, grief. Overall the stolen and repressed memories. Mom was trying to protect me from what happened to me and Gloria, but all she did was make me angry and confused.

Can I be honest with you? I think that's probably the thing I'm most upset about! That my memories were stolen. Yeah, of course I'm angry that I personally was stolen. But my mind was hijacked too. I'm really starting to feel like my life is an episode right out of my favorite show.

Which reminds me, I've really been slacking on the podcast with Nico and Emma! I was listening to old episodes last night while I was awake in bed, and boy, they are so good... You really should listen to them when you have some free time.

"How many waffles *can* you eat?" Max grins after as I shove the last bite in my mouth. We are slouched into a booth at the Waffle House down the block from Dad's gym. The hard yellow bench seats and smell of sweet fake maple syrup is soothing.

"Shmix," I say before I swallow. "Unless you want to give me the rest of yours?" I ask, ogling his plate with two unfinished waffles. He pushes it toward me and I accidentally let out a burp.

We both start laughing.

"Uh... maybe I should be done."

"I know you said you were glad to get out of the house, but I hope you aren't mad about me dragging you here," Max says with a half-smile.

I shake my head and a drop of syrup flings from the side of my lip.

"Good—then hopefully you won't be mad when I tell you to turn around." Max nods at someone behind me. I whip my head around and see Nico and Emma standing there with worried looks on their faces.

"GRACE!" they shout at the same time and jump over the tables and climb into our booth on either side of me. The plates and silverware clank when they bump into the booth. The waitress behind the counter shouts something about how this ain't no jungle gym. But none of us care, and we clench into an awkward but amazing group hug.

"Nico! Emma! God, I missed you both so much." I let them squeeze me as long as they want. I'm not sure how much they've found out about what happened since last time we talked—I overheard Mom and Dad talking outside my door a few nights ago, how pissed off they were to see the story about me and Gloria on the news again. About us being kidnapped twelve years ago. "I'm sorry I haven't messaged back."

"You don't have to be sorry about anything," Nico says and looks me in the eyes. She has pink sparkle stickers around her eyes, and holy shit, is that a nose ring? She winks at me when she sees I notice.

"Yeah, girl, we are here for you no matter what," Emma chimes in. I turn and look at her to see if I missed any other major beauty changes. I scan her face. No piercings. Her hair isn't faded purple anymore, now it's bright aquamarine. I reach a hand up and touch it. "You like? I told my soccer coach he can kiss my ass. If I want to color my hair, I will."

"Really? You said that?"

"Liar," Nico says.

Emma laughs. "Yeah, I just did it yesterday, so Coach hasn't seen it yet. But that's what I'm going to say."

Max chuckles and shakes his head. "If I said something like that to my coach, he'd knock my head off."

"Wait, your coach hits you?" Nico shrieks. "What sport do you even play? I didn't know you were on a team."

"No, not at school. My coach at the gym. I'm training to fight MMA," he explains. Then he looks at his phone. "Crap! I should have been at work almost an hour ago. Your dad's gonna kill me!" He jumps out of the seat. "Meet me over there?" he asks as he runs down the aisle, nearly knocking over the waitress who's coming around with a carafe of coffee. Nico slides around to take up Max's empty seat and holds the cup out for the waitress to fill up.

"No, no, no little missy, I know that weren't your cup. You gotta pay for a new one." The waitress puts her hands on her hip, refusing to fill it up.

Nico pulls two dollars out of her fanny pack and drops it on the table with a grin.

The waitress smirks and fills up the mug.

"For two bucks you think she would have brought you a new cup. Max probably has cooties," I tease. Nico shrugs and takes a sip and makes an exaggerated sighing sound. Then Emma does what I'd been planning to do before I realized how full I was, and she starts eating Max's leftover waffles. I smile.

Is it bad I'd forgotten how nice it was to hang out with my friends? To just sit back and let them chatter about school gossip and funny videos and the latest K-pop that dropped.

"So, Grace," Emma says after she practically licks the plate clean. "Max said he watched you fighting in the gym and that you're pretty good."

"I dunno, I mean when he saw me, I was angry and punching out my feelings."

"That's good. Punching. Fighting. You know, being able to protect yourself. We were kinda thinking we could all go to your dad's gym and practice and talk about our plan," Nico explains.

"What plan?" I wince. Because I might not be feeling myself lately, but I've put the pieces together and I know what my friends are about to say.

"The plan to find Seth and Gloria," Emma says.

I try to take a deep breath, but my lungs close up, making the air hitch painfully... I look around and start to panic.

"Grace, relax. Look, we are going to walk over to the gym and we are going to go inside. Everything is going to be okay. And we will figure this out together." Nico helps me out of the booth and puts her arm around me. "I promise, we will find them."

"But... *What if they're dead*?" I whisper in her ear as she leads me for the door, my feet shuffling along the sticky linoleum checkered tiles.

"No. You and Gloria survived before—"

I don't want her to keep talking about it and I straighten up and shrug her arm off my shoulders before shoving open the Waffle House glass door. The air outside smells like grease and I think I might get sick. A pulsing starts at the nape of my neck, and I know a migraine is coming if I don't do something quick. I bolt into traffic. Nico and Emma scream and a car—no, two cars and a truck—start honking at me. I flip them off as I step onto the sidewalk across the street.

"Grace! Jesus! You've got to watch where you're going." Emma puts her hand on my shoulder after she and Nico catch up to me.

"I'm sorry, I'm about to get a headache. I have to punch it out."

Emma looks at Nico and smiles. "I told you she'd find her inner beast."

Max is behind the front desk when we make it inside, surrounded by a crowd of people buying gloves and signing up for gym memberships. He nods and waves at us as we run through the shop and onto the main floor of the gym.

Electronic music with heavy base is pumping in the gym and there are a ton of guys working out. It's definitely a Saturday—the energy is so high I forget that only moments ago I felt like a pile of shit. What? I told you I was feeling a headache coming on! I guess the waffles and syrup have hit my bloodstream, because I bounce from foot to foot to the beat, balling my hand into a fist and punching my other hand.

"Whoa!" they say at the same time and look around with wide eyes checking out the place. It's the same wonderment I had the last time I was here, well, before my major meltdown. I glance over to the punching bag that I tried killing. It's currently under assault from a guy with arms as big as my thighs. Yikes!

"Let's go to the locker room and we can get suited up. We can take turns punching stuff while we come up with a plan." I skip toward the women's locker room. I'm praying I remember the combination to my old locker, and that Mom left my new gloves in it for me. To my surprise, the numbers come back to me as if I'd been here twirling the dial every day.

Oh, thank God!

Not only are my gloves in the locker, but there's a black gym bag with a ton of new workout clothes stuffed inside with an extra stick of deodorant and some hair ties. The corners of my mouth turn up. Mom. I wonder if that's why she was dressed up this morning—did she go shopping and drop off new clothes for me?

"Looks like there's enough in here for all of us." I toss some stuff at Nico and Emma. We all change quickly. Then I pull my hair up and give myself a once-over in the mirror. I frown at my reflection, I've got huge dark circles under my eyes and my cheeks look hollow. Nico comes up behind me, then Emma. They wrap their arms around me and I look at the image reflecting back.

"We love you," Emma says.

"Yeah, we are gonna get through this together," Nico adds.

Being with my friends lights a spark in me that has been missing all week. I laugh and give them a big squeeze before I spin around.

"Come on, let's go punch something!" I run out of the locker room and onto the gym floor. I go straight for the ring. Not the punching bag.

"Emma, can you hold the strike pads for me? And Nico, I need some help lacing up my gloves." I jump up on the ledge of the boxing ring and shove my body through thick red ropes, like the floor is lava and if I don't get in right now I might burn alive.

"Girl, I love this energy!" Nico says, diving into the ring after me. She holds out the right glove and I slide my hand in, then the left. She tugs them tightly into place and helps me lace them like she's done this a hundred times, even though it's probably her first. Behind her Emma is in position, with the thick strike pads on her hands and as soon as Nico gets out of the way I do a back spin and kick. She has to hold firm not to get knocked over, but she does back up with the pressure from my kick.

"Holy shit, that was intense!" Emma yells and repositions herself and squares up. "Come on Grace, again. Harder." And I do. I spin and kick and follow it with a one-two punch. I focus all of my pent-up anger and energy and go hit after hit. I'm following to the beat of the music, my muscles flex and pull with the highs and lows of the bass and I'm vaguely aware that I'm attracting an audience. Emma puts her hands up for me to stop and she switches out with Nico without asking if I want to keep going. They both know I do.

This is a side of me they rarely see. Maybe they've never seen it, but somehow they are prepared. Like they knew all along that I had this alternate me simmering right under the surface. I suck in the air through my nose in deep pulls and push my bangs back with one arm and wipe the sweat from my eyes.

"I know what to do." I finally stop and take a huge breath. I bend over and exhale. The crowd that's formed around the ring cheers for me and I stand up and take a quick bow. Emma and Nico laugh.

"Well, looks like someone is feeling a little more like herself," a familiar voice says from behind me. The guys have all gone back to their weights and machines. I spin around and see Dad standing there, leaning on the ropes. He looks happy, for the first time in a long time.

"Yeah, well, I guess I just needed my friends to pull me out of the house," I admit.

"See, I told you we could get Grace back," Nico says to my dad.

"That you did, Nico. You and Emma are good friends. Grace is lucky to have you. And since it looks like you kids are having fun, I'm going to head back up to my office to do some paperwork. If you want me to take you to lunch later, just ask before you leave." Dad winks at me then walks over to the end of the gym and up the stairs to his office.

"So, what's the plan?" Emma puts her arm around me. I look over and see Max standing in the doorway of the gym by the shop. He looks anxious.

"Come on, let's go over by Max—he's gonna want to hear this too."

Chapter Fifteen

Amber Alert

"You're out of your mind." Nico shakes her head, her braids swinging side to side.

"What other choice do we have?" I hiss at her. "If the cops aren't going to do shit but sit in their car outside my house, we are going to have to take matters into our own hands!"

"Grace is right, Nico," agrees Emma. If we don't find this prick and get Gloria and Seth back, he's going to kill them. Or keep doing this. I mean, we could be next!" I really hate to think that my friends are worried they will be next, or that Gloria and Seth are going to be murdered.

Then Max's phone makes a loud blaring noise, followed by Nico's and Emma's and mine. Dread forms like a flaming hot ember, burning through my insides.

"Uh, guys—" He looks once at his phone, then takes the remote from the counter and flips off the movie from the screens hanging up around the gym store, switching them to local news.

"What's going on?" I ask, even though I don't have to. I know an Amber Alert alarm. But just for confirmation, I look at the TV. Across the bottom of the screen is one of those scrolling bars: *Local law* *enforcement have issued a statewide **AMBER ALERT** for a missing Richmond Hill teenager.*

I turn around. I can't watch. I don't want to see who else has gone missing.

"Holy shit." Nico reacts first.

"No way. It's Zane Holden!" Emma gasps. My first reaction is that she's faking it. She's so salty that Gloria and Seth are getting all the attention, she's faked her own kidnapping. Except I know in my gut that's not true. I know it's him. It's the rotten-faced man. He's slowly picking off teenagers in Richmond Hill.

"You know Grace, everyone says you and Zane look a lot alike. You don't think he thought it was you?" Max asks. I spin around and glare at Max. How dare he say that! I'm about to tell him what a jerk he is—but then the doors to the gym open and someone comes inside in a hurry.

I think we are all kind of jumpy and Nico and Emma stand in front of me, like I need protecting from whoever it is. I blink a few times and recognize the person as that rude detective lady who was at my house the night Gloria disappeared.

Click.

Tap.

Scratch.

Instinctively I shiver, remembering that horrible ordeal.

Ask Grace... I can hear Gloria's voice, calling out to me. *Ask Grace!*

"Grace Everly, I need you to come with me down to the station," the detective says and walks towards me with her hand outstretched. She elbows Emma and Nico out of the way. "Come with me now," she demands.

When I don't step forward she grabs my arm, her grip like a crab pincer.

"Y'all, wait, no, what's going on?" I slip into a slow southern drawl and make eye contact with Max, pleading with him to help me.

"What the fuck are you doing? Let her go!" Max jumps over the counter like an Olympic gymnast and wedges himself between me and the crustacean.

Whoa! Did you see that? I'm pretty sure she just grew three feet taller, towering over Max and me, with beady black eyes and salty hot breath spewing down on us as she screams.

"I'm Detective Morgenson. Get the hell out of my way, kid. Grace, STATION, NOW!" She shoves Max with her shoulder as she shouts at me.

There are two officers standing outside the gym, watching this mayhem through the glass windows. They both turn around and pretend not to see what's happening.

"Stop, ouch, you're hurting me!"

Detective Morgenson drags me halfway across the gym despite my protesting.

"Detective Morgenson, can I help you?" Dad walks up calmly and puts a hand on her shoulder. She shrinks back to her normal size in an instant, releasing me from her claws. I run back over to Max, using him as my human shield. From the corner of my eye, I see Nico and Emma crouched behind the counter, hiding.

"Mis-ter-Ever-ly." Detective Morgenson says Dad's name in a clipped run-on. "No, you cannot help me. But your daughter can. Zane Holden has been kidnapped and we have reason to believe Grace is involved and—" She spits out the words, but Dad puts his hand up to her face. Yeah, I'm pretty sure his palm is touching the tip of her nose.

"Am I hearing you right? Did you really just march in here and make accusations about my teenage daughter?" Dad practically has steam coming out of his ears.

Morgenson adjusts her suit jacket, tugging at the blue fabric, as she takes a step back from Dad's palm. Then she pulls out that stupid little notebook from her top pocket.

"Would you like to tell me where you were last night, Grace, between the hours of midnight to two a.m.?" She leans to the side to see around Dad and looks at me.

"Grace, don't say a fucking word. This *nice detective* was just leaving. Kids, get to my office," Dad says with a tone I've never heard him use before. I'm not about to wait around to see what happens, so I grab Emma and Nico by the hands and bolt through the doors into the gym and to the back and up the metal stairs, taking them two at a time. Max is right behind us.

"What's going on?" One of Dad's oldest friends, Luke, shouts after us when he sees the panic washed across our faces.

"Cops out front with Dad," I reply as we rush into the office and slam the door. We are panting like we've run a marathon, but it's from the fear and the crazy shit that just happened downstairs.

"OMG, OMG, OMG!" Nico says over and over.

"There's no way this is really happening." Emma shakes her head.

"You can't be serious about what you said downstairs, that you think me and Zane look alike. Right Max?" I ask him. He pushes his hair out of his eyes. I expect to see him shrug and say he was mistaken.

"He's right, you do look alike." Nico pauses her frantic chanting to throw in her two cents. "You're about the same height and you both have that long coppery hair. Of course, she's always dressed like a little slut and you're usually in sweats and a crop. But if someone didn't know either of you very well, they could easily make that mistake."

"God Nico, why didn't you ever tell me before? Maybe I would have cut all my hair off or dyed it like Emma's." I fold my arms over my chest.

"I've got more of this teal color at my house if you wanna," Emma says before throwing herself on the couch.

"Maybe. I've never dyed it before." My brain is trying to protect itself from thinking about what just happened, so I'm hyperfocusing on new hairstyles. I even open my phone and start searching for short, colorful ones.

"Grace, I get that you don't want to look like Zane. But we need to get serious. If the man who kidnapped you and Gloria back in the day is the same person who took Gloria, Seth, and now Zane, it's only a matter of time before he comes back." Nico sits down in my dad's desk chair.

I look up from my phone and stare at her.

"Once he figures out Zane isn't you, he'll come back. He could end up taking me or Emma in the process of getting to you," she says.

"Hell no." I shake my head.

She stands up and slams her hands on Dad's desk. Emma squeaks.

"That's right! Hell no! So, what are we going to do about this?" Nico wants to be a lawyer someday, and I know she will; just look at her behind a desk, staring at all of us in the eyes and demanding the truth. But if these kidnappings don't stop—

Nico is right. Any one of us could be next. And then what?

Max whispers what we are all thinking, "If we don't stop him—we are all dead."

Chapter Sixteen

WE'RE SITTING DUCKS

Dad flings open the door to his office. The wood and glass make a popping noise when the door slams against the wall and we all scream and jump.

"Jesus, Dad, are you trying to give us all a heart attack?"

"Sorry, Grace." He rubs his hands over his face. "Detective Morgenson finally left. But she's out for blood. I don't know why she thinks *you* are involved with these disappearances, but we are not going to sit around and find out. You and your friends need to get back to the house and call your parents."

Emma, Nico, and Max rally around me and we put our heads together, like we are coming up with some kind of Hail Mary in the last two seconds of the game. I can feel Emma's knees shaking.

"It's gonna be okay," I whisper.

"I'm heading down to the police station right now, if I can convince Luke to go with me," Dad says. "He's an attorney. I want to have a little conversation with the Police Chief regarding the harassment of a minor." He shuffles papers around on his desk and bangs around in the drawers.

"I don't think we should go to my house, the cops are probably waiting there for me," I hiss to my friends.

"Well, what are you four waiting for? Max, I'll pay you for the rest of the day. Don't worry about that. I can get Toby to cover the front." Dad's arms are full of God knows what and he flies like a wasp out of his office.

"Where should we go then?" Emma asks. We back out of our huddle formation now that Dad's gone.

"Let's just stay here," Nico suggests.

"No, Grace is right. Detective Morgenson might come back here. Or Grace's house. There's only one place we can go," Max says. He cracks his knuckles, then his neck. "My house. We can park in the alley behind the fence and hang out in my shed."

"Your shed, uh, no." Nico's face twists up.

"It's not gross. It's where I game. My mom hated me yelling in the house, so last summer I turned it into my hangout spot."

I imagine a dusty old potting shed with an even dustier old couch, a mini-fridge filled with soda, and a bunch of video games stacked up next to the TV. I can practically taste the Cheetos now.

"Sounds perfect, let's go."

***

The inside of Max's shed is actually a lot nicer than I imagined, with a decent couch and a full-sized fridge filled with soda and bottled waters. Which is a good thing, since we might be here for a while. I didn't want our parents to worry, so we each texted that we were at someone else's house, so if our parents call one another it will take them some time to figure it out. I can practically hear Mom now: *The girls? They said they were at Emma's house.*

"Grace, when you were boxing in the ring, you said you'd come up with a plan. Do you want to share with the group?" Nico being Nico.

I shake my head and chuckle nervously.

I honestly don't know what I was thinking when I was fighting.

My adrenaline was so high—I had this bright idea that if we did another one of our *What's in the Woods* podcasts, that maybe we could lure out the rotten-faced man and then capture him. But that's so stupid. I mean, why would he be listening to our podcast?

It does give me a different idea, though. "What if we start podcasting this? Gloria's disappearance, the kidnapping when we were kids, Seth, Zane, the note. All of it."

"Do you really want everyone on the internet to know your whole life?" Max asks, shaking his head no. "Those true-crime people get really caught up in it. We could end up with a thousand weirdos coming to town to try and crack the case. People could get hurt." He gazes at the ceiling as if he is imagining people with pitchforks circling our town and he shivers.

"Yeah, that's true," Emma agrees. "I can see it now, people with guns in the streets, harassing anyone who looks a little strange."

Ugh, they're right. Doing a podcast episode could just put everyone in even more danger.

"Okay, so maybe I don't have a plan." I slump further back into the couch. I feel ashamed of myself. I wish I knew what to do! I wish I knew *who* the rotten-faced man was, so I could just tell everyone how to find him. It has to be him, right? The man who took me and Gloria has to be the person responsible for these kidnappings? My skin is itching and the air wraps around me like my blanket suffocating me when I sleep.

"Max, it's really hot in here," I whine.

"Oh, sorry, I forgot to flip on the air," he says and flicks the switch on the swamp cooler. It rumbles loudly as it comes alive to cool the air in my lungs.

Then Nico stands up and does that thing when she's deep in thought: she kind of lunge-walks with her hands on her hips, pausing every now and again. "Oh... no." She shakes her head and lunges a few more steps, spins and walks the other way.

"Can't we just turn on a movie while you brainstorm? Does it have to be the lunges?" Emma asks. Max seems to agree, because he grabs the remote.

"Grace, you're a genius!" Nico shouts.

"Uh, that was my idea, not Grace's, to put on a movie. And yeah, Mom always says my IQ is above average."

"No, not the movie." Nico rolls her eyes. "That thing Grace said, about sharing the story on our podcast. Max is right—people go nuts over true crime documentaries. So what if we tell the story about Grace but use different information?" Nico is getting more and more hyped up as she says it. She's stopped lunging and is now bouncing from foot to foot. She looks like she's got mini trampolines strapped to her feet.

"Uh, I don't get it." Emma scratches her head. I stifle a giggle, because, well, Emma is cute when she's confused.

"We turn it into a COLD CASE. Like we tell the story, but pretend it happened thirty years ago or something. We give one of those whatchamacallits, 'to protect the families involved in this cold case, names have been changed' or, uh, I dunno."

"You mean a disclaimer."

"Yeah! A disclaimer!" Nico yells.

I think about it. God, I really hate cop shows. And it looks like instead of doing our fun weekly podcast about make-believe monsters in the woods, we are gonna be talking about—oh wait. We'll still be talking about monsters in the woods, because the rotten-faced man is a monster. That is, if he's the one who's been doing the kidnapping. There is still the possibility that it's someone else in town...

Nico is right.

We need help.

Chapter Seventeen

THE SCARIEST PODCAST EVER!

It takes us a few days to set up a podcasting studio in Max's shed. We borrow a table from Emma's house, some extra chairs from Nico's garage, and some blankets from my house to help with soundproofing.

It feels good to have something else to focus on besides the terrors running free inside of my brain. Nico, Emma, and Max haven't given me a second of time to myself. Emma and Nico have stayed at my house the last two nights with permission from their parents, and no, smartass, we didn't get caught lying about our location the other day after Detective Morgensen clenched my arm like the Jaws of Life. Dad was too distracted to even remember to tell Mom we were supposed to be on our way home. He marched his ass right down to the police station and threatened a lawsuit so big it would make their heads explode.

Have I mentioned that sometimes it's nice to have a big, muscle-bound dude as a dad? Because, well, it is nice. I've always felt safe and protected when my dad is around. I know he would do anything to keep me safe. Including being thrown in jail himself for screaming at the Chief of Police over unacceptable treatment of a minor.

And guess what?

The Chief put Detective Morgensen on administrative leave for her little stunt. Not that he took Dad's word for it. No, he watched the security footage from the gym and decided all on his own that the detective was *waaaaaay* out of line.

Oh, and another thing, with all these kidnappings, the school district came to the wise decision last night and canceled school for the week! Well... my mom might have had something to do with that. She rallied her social media friends with a call to action and set up a huge protest outside the houses of each school board member. While me and my friends have spent two days building a new recording studio at Max's house instead of our makeshift haunt in Nico's closet, our moms have been waving signs and chanting *PROTECT OUR KIDS! CLOSE THE SCHOOLS!*

Thanks to Mom and her friends, word about what happened to Gloria, Seth, and Zane started spreading around town. Especially the fact that Gloria had been snatched from school property. A little detail they'd first withheld from the public, but now...

Remember how I thought it was strange they had no security footage of Gloria?

It was like she'd walked out of school and just disappeared off the face of the Earth?

I mean, stranger things have happened?

Yeah, well not in this case. That Kwik Stop gas station with the stoners and smokers across the street from school? They aren't complete morons and finally found the footage from that day, stored on the hard drive at their corporate office in Atlanta.

According to their security camera footage, Gloria wasn't snatched out of thin air. First, she walked across the street and bought a pack of spearmint gum and a bottle of water. She was even smiling and said "thank you" to the cashier. That tall, dark haired, porcelain-faced mute just wanted a pack of gum and something to drink? Are you kidding me? Like she couldn't have asked a thousand kids at school, who all would have handed over gum and water.

And just her luck. As she crossed the street, heading back to school—I mean come on Gloria, if you're gonna skip, why go back to class? Anyway, it was just her luck that a dark van, without any visible markings, pulled up and stole her right off the school sidewalk. It only took three seconds. Three stupid, insignificant seconds to change the entire course of my existence.

Throw in the fact that Seth went missing two days later, and Zane a week after that, and now every teenager in town is scared to leave their house.

Every parent in town is scared too.

And that's why they closed the school.

Well, that and my mom.

"You guys want to do a test run?" Max asks as he closes the last black plastic zip tie to hold our microphone wires in place. His shed has been completely transformed into a much better recording studio than Nico's closet or my laundry room, which houses our cat's litter box. With the army of blankets covering the walls and windows, and Christmas lights twinkling, it feels like we are in a club house. All we need is a sign outside that says *No Grown-Upz Allowed!* I love it, if I'm being totally honest, because it feels safe and comfortable and a world away from what is happening outside the shed.

And what exactly is happening?

Well, we found out more about Zane Holden's kidnapping. It's been all over TikTok, and on every video that gets posted, someone from school tags me. Apparently it isn't just my friends who made the connection that Zane looks like me.

Am I the only person who didn't see it?

I wonder if Zane realized we looked alike. If she had, I wonder if she would have changed her hair or her makeup to look less like me. Knowing her, she would have tried to bully me into cutting off my hair instead.

Anyway, according to all the videos, Zane told her mom she had to go meet up with a friend. Her mom assumed it was either Dani or Sarah. But Dani and Sarah told the police neither of them asked her to meet them, because Sarah was at a Show Choir performance in Savannah and Dani was having a late dinner with her parents and brother out in Hinesville. So who was Zane meeting?

Well, the police—or should I say Detective Morgensen—got it in her pea-sized brain that it must have been me. For reasons I can't understand, she thinks I lured Zane out of her house so the kidnapper could take her. More likely she was meeting up with a secret boyfriend. Who knows. But obviously it wasn't me.

The video I found most upsetting was one posted by, you guessed it, 7TRUTHZ. It was just a picture of Zane, with an AI voice narrating.

Zane Holden was taken by an evil spirit.

An evil spirit wearing the face of Grace Everly.

Look at the facts.

Grace's best friend, Gloria. Taken.

Grace's boyfriend, Seth. Taken.

Grace's enemy, Zane. Taken.

Do you know Grace Everly? Watch your back.

And then, just for shock value, the picture of Zane switched to a really disgusting picture of me at school with my eyes half closed, mid-sentence, in the hallway. Who even took that picture? The words *YOU'RE NEXT* flashed big and red with bloody splotches dripping down the screen.

Whoever made that video knows how to use CapCut on TikTok. So it's got to be someone at school. But seriously, not cool. Really fucking annoying, to be honest. Don't even get me started on all the hater comments accusing me of being a devil worshiper, kidnapper accomplice, and worse.

"Stop doomscrolling." Nico puts her hand on my shoulder.

"It's not like I want to! But everyone is tagging me in all these stupid videos. I mean, are people dumb enough to think I'm involved in their disappearances?" I slump in my chair and hastily pull my hair back with the scrunchie I'd been wearing as a bracelet.

"I doubt anyone thinks you're involved, Grace. They're just making assumptions. That's why you're doing the podcast. Remember? To tell your side of the story. To put the truth out there," Max says. Then he fidgets around on his computer. "I'm ready if you guys are. We should start recording if you want it to go up at eight, like we planned."

I guess I'm as ready as I'll ever be to tell our story, mine and Gloria's. I still don't know everything that happened to us. And I'm not sure I will ever remember all of it, since I spent years of my life being trained to forget. My memories keep coming back in bits and pieces, enough to do our podcast, but it doesn't mean that it's going to help our investigation.

Maybe no one can help us.

What's in the Woods?

ME: *Hey all you nerds. Welcome to another episode of—*

NICO, EMMA & ME (All together): *What's in the Woods?*

Max plays a creepy music sequence he put together this afternoon. We didn't even ask him to do it, but seriously it's perfect for our show. Hopefully he will let us keep it to use from now on.

EMMA (laughing): *Oooh, love the new intro music, super scary, thanks Max! It's so perfect for today's episode.*

NICO (leaning into her microphone, her voice dropping an octave): *And why's that, Emma?*

EMMA: *Because today, on What's in the Woods?, we aren't just telling a story we made up. Today we are telling a true story about something that happened in the woods.*

ME (heart pounding, this is it, I have one shot to make the audience want to help us find Gloria, Max, and Zane): *That's right. We have cracked open a real-life cold case file. Of course, the names have been changed to protect the families. But this story is as dark as they come, and today we want your help to solve the mystery of What's in the Woods?*

I pause, sweat dripping down my brow as I look at the script we hastily threw together with the facts about Gloria, Seth, and Zane's disappearance. We changed the names, but my eyes can't focus. I set down the paper and rub my face. Nico sees me spiraling and jumps in.

NICO: *Ooooh, Grace, this sounds intriguing. Can you tell us more?*

She's waving her hand and mouthing, *Are you okay?*

I nod, take a deep breath, and do something that my friends will probably kill me for later. That is, if the kidnapper doesn't find me and kill me first.

ME: *You know what? We had this big plan, we were going to call this a cold case and change the names and ask for help. But that's stupid. Why should we have to hide what's happening in Richmond Hill?*

Max's eyes bug out and he shakes his head no. Emma is making a cut motion across her throat. Nico looks over and sees Emma and chucks a gummy worm at her.

ME: *I know you can't see what's going on here, but my friends are panicking. See, they are afraid that if we tell the world what's happening* *here, well—maybe it will make things worse. Maybe it will cause this monster to strike again.*

EMMA (with genuine fear in her voice): *You don't really think he's going to strike again, do you, Grace?*

ME (sighing heavily into the microphone): *Yes, Emma. That's why we are doing this. To warn everyone and to get more people to help us find Gloria, Seth, and Zane, since the cops aren't doing a damn thing.*

Emma winks at me. Oh, that sneaky girl, she set me up for that one. And now that I've said their names, there is no going back; the words bubble up at my lips, like a swollen river after the snow melts in spring.

ME: *That's right. Three teenagers in Richmond Hill have gone missing. Stolen, right out from under the noses of our small town. Without a trace. And not just any three teenagers... My next-door neighbor Gloria, my boyfriend Seth, and a girl in our grade who looks just like me, Zane.*

NICO: *Do you think the kidnapper was coming for you but accidentally took Zane?*

ME: *Yeah, I do.*

NICO: *Why would someone be doing this to you?*

ME: *Because this isn't the first time a monster has found its way to Richmond Hill to steal children.*

Emma shivers, even though it's humid in the shed no matter how high Max has his swamp cooler turned up. I don't blame her. We have a monster loose in our town.

ME: *I was taken by the monster when I was four. Not just me. Me and Gloria. We were kidnapped, lured out of the park by a puppy chasing a blue ball.*

I close my eyes, remembering that day. The sun on my face, my hair floating as I ran with Gloria, our arms out like we were flying. The joy in our hearts, because we were having so much fun. Until the man. Gloria's scream echoes in my mind.

ME (I keep my eyes closed and describe what happened): *A man, wearing overalls. I call him the rotten-faced man because he had leathery tan skin from being in the sun and scars over one side of his face—like a chemical burn.*

I sniff the air, trying to remember what he smelled like the first time he grabbed me.

ME: *He smelled like gasoline and peanut butter.*

NICO: *So this peanut-farmer freak show kidnapped you and Gloria? Did he hurt you?*

ME: *Not exactly. He locked us in a dog cage, next to other cages filled with puppies. My memories are really blurry about the entire thing. Which is a topic for another day. But what matters is that we escaped and the police found us wandering along the highway like a hundred miles from here.*

EMMA (whispers into her mic): *The monster has returned to Richmond Hill to take revenge on Grace and Gloria.*

This time it's Max who throws a gummy worm at Emma. She ducks and the gummy sails over her head. She pops back up and grabs her mic again.

EMMA: *What? It's true, guys! Who else could it be?*

ME: *But why would he want revenge on us? He wasn't found! He was never arrested.*

EMMA: *Because you escaped. He has unfinished business with you. Who else could it be?*

NICO: *Maybe it's a copycat?*

EMMA (glaring at Nico): *Copycat? This many years later? How would anyone even know about what happened to Gloria and Grace?*

I mean, we are Grace's best friends and we didn't even know she'd been kidnapped when she was little!

NICO: *That's not fair. Grace didn't even know she'd been kidnapped until a few—*

ME (interrupting): *Okay, okay, before we get into the topic of my memories, let's wrap this episode up. We've laid out the facts for all you listeners. There is a monster on the loose in Richmond Hill. Gloria, Seth, and Zane have been kidnapped, without a ransom letter or any contact with authorities that we know of. Gloria and I were kidnapped when we were kids and the person who did it was never caught.*

I pause and take a deep breath before I continue.

Max is going to post a link to the official What's in the Woods? email account so anyone who is listening can send in tips. We need your help to find Gloria, Seth, and Zane before it's...

But I can't bring myself to say it. Thankfully, Nico sees me tearing up and jumps in to finish the episode before I start bawling and ruin the entire thing.

NICO: *Uh, yeah, if you have any knowledge about the whereabouts of our friends, please email us. Max, take it away.*

Max plays the spooky music again, then gives us all the signal when he hits the button, ending the episode. He takes his headphones off and sets them down gently.

"Grace, are you okay? That was—" He pauses. "Uh, guys, I think uh..."

PING. PING. PING. Max's computer starts making all kinds of noises.

"Max, what the heck is that?" Nico asks. "And Grace, you did a great job. You too Emma, sorry about all the gummy worms." But Emma's mouth is full of sugar and she just grins and nods.

"That," Max starts, but is immediately interrupted by more PING, PING, PINGing, "is the alert I set on my computer to make sure we didn't miss any leads being emailed in. Looks like we had more than a few listeners on the podcast."

I leap from my seat and run over to look at Max's computer screen. Nico is maneuvering her body next to me so she can see the screen, while Emma is jumping up and down behind us trying to catch a glimpse. We adjust our positioning so Emma can see, and then we all gasp when Max opens up the inbox.

"Oh my God, there's already twenty messages? Do you think any of them are credible?" I ask. I thought maybe we'd get one or two later tonight, but twenty within five minutes of the show ending? The hair on the back of my neck stands on edge. I'm not sure I'm prepared to see what kind of messages our listeners have sent. What if there are others like me and Gloria—people who were kidnapped and escaped? What if there's information? Maybe more security footage of Gloria or maybe someone saw what happened to Seth. Or it could just be hate mail from Zane's friends and family.

My entire body tightens. I'm frightened and I'm not sure I can look.

"Only one way to find out," Max says and clicks to open the first email.

Just as the email opens, our faces awash in the computer screen glow, my stomach makes a super rude growly noise and everyone laughs. "Maybe we should order some pizza, I think this is gonna be a long night," I say. I step away from the screen, partially because I really am too scared to read the messages and partially because I'm starving.

A nice, greasy, hot, cheese pizza from Rosie's Pizza Cafe is the only thing that's going to do the trick right now. So, instead of just one,

I'm going to order two. Mmmm... my mouth salivates thinking about food.

"Uh, Grace, I think you need to see this..." Nico says over her shoulder as I finish placing the pizza order on my phone.

"I need food first. I can't deal with it on an empty stomach."

Nico and Emma exchange glances, then they pull up their chairs to sit by Max to keep looking at the emails. While I, on the other hand, go lie on the couch and scroll through pictures of me and Seth.

Chapter Eighteen

HE'S ALREADY DEAD

The pizza really does hit the spot. I kick my legs out on the couch and stretch my toes, staring at the episode of *Stranger Things* we turned on for some distraction while we ate. Yes. All right, maybe I am stalling. But just give me a few more minutes. I want to find my friends, but I'm also terrified to learn more about what happened to me and Gloria. Wouldn't you be?

Finally, when I can tell my friends are getting antsy and the vibe in the air is like static electricity ready to pop off at any second, I announce, "Okay. I'm ready. What did the emails say?" It's time to get down to business.

Max is back at the computer as soon as I give the green light. "Oh my God, there's been another fifty messages while we ate." He whistles long and low.

"No way! We've never had that many listeners or comments before... Are we going viral?" Emma asks.

Exactly what I thought would happen. It's just a matter of time before our town is filled with monster hunters and vigilantes looking for justice for Gloria, Seth, and Zane. What have I done? My cheeks feel damp with sweat when I put my hands up to cradle my face in despair.

"Okay, so Grace, the thing we saw before pizza—I'm not sure how to tell you this, but someone sent information about the man they think was your kidnapper. It seems pretty credible." Max looks over his shoulder at me.

My heart beats wildly. That fast? Someone figured out who the man who kidnapped us was that freaking fast? I'm struggling to even remember what I said during the podcast. How did I describe him? Was it enough? Or is someone just messing with me?

"No," I say and cross my arms in defiance. I mean, yes. I want him to be found. But—how could it be this easy? "It's probably a troll," I add, so my friends know why I said no.

Nico comes up behind me and rubs my shoulders.

I try my hardest not to flinch from her touch. I know she's just trying to help, but I'm not in the mood for anyone to be this close to me.

"Not a troll. It's an email from a Richmond Hill librarian, Ms. Kemper, with a link to an article about a man killed in a car crash on Highway 12. That's where you and Gloria were found wasn't it?" Max asks.

I involuntarily gag and clutch my stomach.

There's an article? About our kidnapper? How does the fucking librarian know it's him? My skin is crawling and my limbs are Jello. But I manage to drag myself off the couch and stumble to the computer where Max has the article pulled up. I squint and try to read the words, but my vision is blurry, my mouth feels dry, and I can't focus on anything.

"I can't read it," I mumble.

Nico joins us, and she begins reading the article out loud, using a very low and even-tempered voice. As if she's reading a chapter of a *Goosebumps* book hoping to make us scream when they find the swamp monster.

Eustis Roland Orr, a local peanut farmer, died after he lost control of his truck speeding northbound on Highway 12 early Wednesday morning, according to the Charlton County Sheriff's Office.

The sheriff's office received a 911 call about the crash at 3:16 a.m. Wednesday. Deputies found Orr, 54, of Waycross, at the scene. He was the only person in the truck, according to the sheriff's office. However, Orr had several crates of dogs in his possession, all unhurt, and they've been transferred to the local Humane Society for adoption.

Orr's truck left the north side of the road at the curve in the road near the Okefenokee Swamp route. He hit a utility pole, fencing along the road, and a second utility pole before the truck came to a stop, according to the sheriff's office.

An autopsy is scheduled for Friday, Charlton County Coroner Aubrie Seton said.

And there's a picture.

A picture of Eustis Roland Orr.

My stomach clenches, and I'm positive I'm going to barf. A peanut farmer? Crates of dogs? I can't take my eyes off him. I've seen him a thousand times in my nightmares. They all come flooding back to me, in a horrible barrage.

"Is that him?" Emma asks.

I can't speak. I can only nod my head up and down. I manage to make my way back to the couch and flop down, shoving my face into a scratchy throw pillow, before I start screaming.

Chapter Nineteen

THE SOUND OF SILENCE

I 've composed myself while Max, Nico, and Emma read through all of the tips, emails, and comments on our podcast. And yeah, it's gone viral.

My phone is blowing up too, but I can't stand to look at it.

Most of the comments are crap. People saying we're faking it. Others claiming the same thing happened to them. And then there's the accusers... women saying it sounds like something their ex-husband would do. Men accusing their girlfriends. Layer that with the long list of people telling us their personal experiences with monsters, werewolves, vampires, basically anything that goes bump in the night, and wow.

I wonder if this is what happens on police hotlines. Do they get inundated with thousands of nonsense tips and have to sort through them like a needle in the haystack for the singular one of value?

"Turn it off." My voice is barely above a whisper. "I mean, delete it. Delete the podcast." I get louder this time.

"Why?" Nico asks.

"Because it's pointless! Are you even listening to all of that bullshit?" I'm tired and as my mom likes to say, I've got my crabby pants on. "Our only real lead was the article about the rotten-faced man, Eustis." I cough as I try to say his name. "And he's dead."

I don't want to use his real name; he doesn't deserve to have a name.

Not after what he did to me and Gloria.

Emma comes over and sits down next to me. I let my body soften and lean into her, resting my head on her shoulder. A wailing in the distance makes everyone go silent, as if we are holding our breath, until the police sirens racing down the street finally pass by Max's house. Our makeshift studio in the shed felt so safe and secure when we started this thing, but now it doesn't feel safe. Nowhere is safe.

Max rubs his sandy-blond hair, as if it's going to give him a new idea. He opens his mouth once to say something, closes it, then opens it again. "Let's take a step back and look at the facts from the beginning. You said Gloria left a note on her desk the morning she was kidnapped that said *Ask Grace*."

"Yeah," I grumble.

"Well, maybe she actually wanted to ask you something. Maybe it was just a reminder to herself, not a message for the police to find. Not a super clue to unlock Pandora's box," Max says.

"You mean my brain?" I ask.

"Max is right. It doesn't make any sense, how would Gloria know she was going to be kidnapped?" Nico twirls a piece of her dark hair on her finger, wrapping it over and over around her green-and-blue-striped nails.

I sit up. "As if anything Gloria did made any sense. She completely ignored me all the time," I complain.

"That's not true. She didn't ignore you. She was with you every day, she just didn't talk. I mean, now that you remember that the two of you were kidnapped together as kids, maybe you could cut her some slack." Emma gives me a look. "I mean, it was probably too painful for her. She didn't have her memories erased like you did."

Emma points out something I hadn't even considered. Oh my God. She's right! Gloria didn't have a second-cousin therapist named Tammy in her life to flay her mind and erase all her memories like she was a lab rat. She was living every single day with the knowledge of what happened to us, and she never said a word about it.

"She never said a word about it," I whisper. "She. Never. Said. A. Word!"

"Uh, Grace?" Max asks.

I'm so excited that I finally understand. Gloria didn't hate me! She was terrified that if she said anything to me, a single word, that she'd tell me everything that happened when we were kids and I'd remember. And if I remembered, then maybe I'd talk about it—and worse, I might talk about it with her. Gloria wasn't just protecting me from my own memories, *she was protecting herself.*

My mind is moving a million miles a minute. Did her mom come up with this idea not to talk to me? Or my mom? I mean, I get it now, that it was a way of self-preservation. But something doesn't feel right about it. Just like it doesn't feel right that Tammy used her techniques to mess with my mind and make me forget what happened.

"Emma, you're a genius!" I grab her up in a hug.

"Really?" Nico smirks.

"Oh, shove it Nico." Emma sticks her tongue out.

"We need to go see Gloria's mom. Start at the beginning, right?" I put my shoes on as fast as I can. That's when the hair on my neck stands up at the sound of sirens again, far away but growing closer. Not just a single police car, at least three or four, and maybe an ambulance. The neighborhood dogs howl and I flinch.

"That doesn't sound good," Max says. His keys jingle as he puts them in his pocket and flicks off his computer. Just as he's about to unplug the Christmas lights we strung up in our makeshift studio, I reach out and grab his arm. His skin is warm and a little sticky. He looks at me, eyebrows knitted.

"Can we leave the lights on? I have a feeling we'll be back later. And a dark shed in the middle of the night—sounds like the scene from *Texas Chainsaw Massacre*."

"Right. Leave the lights on. Good call, Grace." Max smiles.

I check my phone. Nine-thirty. Hopefully Mrs. Sanchez is still awake.

"You guys ready?" Nico opens the door, and we step out into the humid night air. Heading to the beginning, a place we might find something, anything, that will help us figure out who took Gloria and Seth.

My heart aches. I have to find them. I have to tell them how much I love them both.

Chapter Twenty

Our Hands Were Tied

"Should we park in the alley?" I ask Max as he turns his car into my neighborhood. I doubt those cops are still outside my house, but you never know. Plus, Mom and Dad like to watch TV this time of night, and the living room is at the front of the house. Mom is the kind of nosey neighbor who gets up and looks out the window when she sees car lights parking on the street. I told her I was spending the night at Emma's house, which means she might not appreciate me roaming the neighborhood with my friends after dark while there's a kidnapper on the loose.

"But won't we look suspicious, sneaking around in the alley and walking up to Gloria's back door?" Emma asks from the backseat. "We might scare the crap out of her parents."

"Ugh, yeah, you're probably right. I just don't want my mom to see us, so we should park on the other side of Gloria's house," I say.

Max nods. He veers to the left and then makes the right turn on my street and slams on the brakes. A line of cars is blocking the entire road in both directions, the red taillights lighting up the night. "What the hell is this?"

"I'd say we've got lookie-loos," Emma says. She and Nico lean forward over the center console, putting their heads in the middle between the front seats to get a better view.

"Alley parking it is," Max says. He puts the car in reverse before we can get blocked in, backs up, then steps on the gas going around our block and coming in through the back alley. Thankfully it's dark and pretty empty, except for trash cans and junk.

Max inches his car down the narrow lane, pulling in front of Gloria's parents' garage. There really isn't anywhere to park, and Max says, "You better get out here, I'll go find a place to park and—"

"NO!" Nico, Emma, and I all scream at the same time. Max jumps in his seat.

"Whoa, why the freak-out?"

"Hello? Have you forgotten there is still a kidnapper on the loose? You're not going anywhere alone. Just park here. Who cares if we block the alley," I tell him.

"Yeah, okay, sorry." Max rubs his face.

We all pile out of his car and quickly go through the back gate and up to Gloria's back door. The porch light is on and the house is pretty well lit. I guess her parents are awake. I knock once, then twice, and as I'm about to knock a third time, the door flies open.

"Grace! What are you doing outside? Hurry, get in quickly, are you kids okay? Has something happened?" Mrs. Sanchez is wide-eyed. Thankfully she's not in her pajamas. The kitchen smells like a fresh pot of coffee. I wonder if she isn't sleeping much these days, staying up waiting for any news on Gloria. It's been two weeks. Two long weeks since Gloria has been taken. I try not to let my mind think about what that means for her... considering we are long past the first forty-eight hours.

"Thank you. And we're okay." I reassure Mrs. Sanchez that we aren't hurt or in trouble, but the look on her face says she doesn't really believe me. "You remember Nico and Emma. And this is Max. He's *friends* with Gloria too." I don't want to blow up Gloria's spot, even if she is missing.

"I'm glad to hear you're okay. But Grace, I'm sure you didn't come just to have a cup of coffee with me this late, so why don't you kids take a seat and tell me what's really going on," she says and pours herself a fresh cup of steaming coffee and motions for us to sit around the kitchen table.

The front door opens and closes, and after a few seconds, Mr. Sanchez walks in. "Daisy, I was over talking to Mark, sounds like Grace and her friends did a podcast—" He pauses when he sees us. "Oh, Grace. I wasn't expecting you. Is everything okay?"

"Um, yes. No. I mean." My bottom lip quivers when I stare at Gloria's parents. She looks so much like them—the dark hair and brown eyes, her dad's height, her mom's sloped nose. And now that I know she didn't really hate me and was just trying to protect me from my own mind, I feel really shitty that I stopped coming over here on Friday nights. My parents stopped coming over too. Why did I have to ruin it for everyone?

"Sweetheart, don't cry," Mrs. Sanchez says.

I have to look away, because the hot tears are rolling down my cheeks and I can't stop them. Nico and Emma lean into me and grab my hands; they both start whispering that everything is fine, and they've got me.

It's Max who steps up to explain.

"Hey, um, hi Mr. and Mrs. Sanchez—I'm Max. I'm friends with Gloria, like Grace said. I want to help find her and Seth and Zane..." He pauses. "Look, Grace finally remembered what happened to her and Gloria, about the man who kidnapped them. So we did a podcast, to try and figure out who he is, because we thought he must have come back to take Gloria." Max stops to take a breath.

Mr. Sanchez stiffens.

And Mrs. Sanchez comes over and puts her arms around me. "Oh, Grace honey, you remember? I'm so, so sorry about what happened to you girls. Gloria wanted to talk to you about it. But your mom's cousin Tammy, she didn't want you to remember what happened. Our hands were tied." Then she shakes her head vigorously. "Uh, scratch that last bit. Bad analogy."

I laugh a little.

"It's okay. And from what I remember, there were no hands tied. Just smelly dog cages."

"That's why we're here, Mrs. Sanchez. We thought it was him. The rotten-faced man who kidnapped Gloria again. But after our podcast, we got a tip from a listener, and—" Emma has her phone out and pulls up the article the librarian sent us after our podcast aired. She hands it over and Gloria's parents lean in, shoulder-to-shoulder, reading the article quickly.

"This man, you believe he's the one who kidnapped you and Gloria when you were children?" Mrs. Sanchez asks. She looks like she's seen a ghost.

"I do. I've had nightmares with that face. And the description fits. Peanut farmer, dogs. So, if he's dead, then someone else took Gloria, Seth, and Zane. We were hoping we could look in Gloria's room again at the note. We have to start investigating from the beginning."

"Daisy, we need to get this information to the police. If this was him..." Mr. Sanchez is distracted. Mrs. Sanchez has her own phone out, and she's dialing a phone number.

"Waaaay ahead of you, I'm calling the station right now." She starts walking out of the kitchen, toward another room. "Oh, Grace. Um, yes. You kids can go up to Gloria's room."

We don't have to be told twice. The chairs screech as we all get up in unison.

"Take off your shoes," I hiss at everyone when we get out to the front entry. I'm sure we sound like a herd of elephants charging up the stairs toward Gloria's room in our sock feet. This time I know what to expect and I'm not worried about finding a cauldron of bubbling witch's brew or shelves of black candles or a pentagon on the floor.

Just a normal, teenage bedroom.

Max hesitates in the hallway, after Nico and Emma pile into Gloria's room.

"What are you waiting for?" I ask.

"I mean, I like her, you know… is it weird if I'm in her bedroom?"

I smile and shake my head. Awwww. How cute. Max finally admitted that he likes Gloria. Maybe she never used to talk to me, but once we get that doll-face back, she better talk to me! Because I'm gonna want all the juicy details of this relationship with Max. I can see the sparkle in his eyes every time he talks about her. He really does like her.

Finally, after a deep breath, he hesitantly enters her room. His back is stiff as a board, but his shoulders relax once he's inside. I know that feeling.

Now, it's time to get down to business.

"Sorry Gloria, but I'm going to go through all your shit," I say into the air. Nico and Emma stifle a laugh, but Max nods once with approval.

Chapter Twenty-One

GONE. JUST GONE.

We spend thirty minutes going through Gloria's room. Checking her stacks of books for notes in the margins, flipping through all the papers in her desk, looking in boxes under her bed, anything we can think of to find a clue about what happened to her.

But we find nothing, other than the original note.

Ask Grace.

I want to crumple it up and throw it in the little pink trash basket under her desk. But that would be destroying evidence, so I leave it there. I sit down on the edge of Gloria's bed, rubbing my temples. This is so frustrating.

Right? I mean, aren't you pulling your hair out by now?

Why couldn't she have left some long manifesto letter detailing exactly what the hell is going on? Because... When I really think about Gloria, like who she is, who I've always known her to be, she's not some erratic psychopath.

She's tidy, organized, and even colorful. She's in goddamned show choir! Just look at her stupid desk filled with color-coded containers of pens and beads and art supplies. She has notes and drawings and all kinds of poems. There isn't time to read all of them, but from flipping through, I can tell she's into some pretty cool shit.

Then there's the boxes of pictures of film negatives.

Apparently she's into photography. Who knew?

I flip through a stack of pictures. Mostly nature shots—the sunlight shining through trees, flowers, that kind of stuff. I shuffle the pictures looking for anything else. I find a few pictures of tile mosaics made from scraps. Her dad, Rafael, owns a tile company downtown, so she must have access to all kinds of bits and pieces. Gloria is so creative. I'd never have thought to make anything like this. I set the pictures down, looking in the next box. It's full of developed film negatives. I hold one of the film strips up to the light and smile. It's a picture of a cat dipping its paw into a koi pond, the fish visible at the surface.

But what's kinda strange is she doesn't have a camera or a computer. I don't see cords or plugs or anything else laying around that might indicate she keeps tech in her room. I wonder if it's downstairs somewhere.

Emma, Nico, and Max are busy chatting.

Ugh, it sucks hitting another dead end! If the rotten-faced man is dead. Then why did Gloria leave me that note? What was she going to ask me? Think, damn it! I start pacing around, trying to come up with anything that makes sense.

"Maybe the clues aren't here. Maybe we need to go to Seth's house. He was taken next—" Max says, interrupting my pacing.

Seth! Oh God, Seth. I've been so focused on the Gloria angle, I practically forgot about my missing boyfriend. I thought this was linked to me somehow. First Gloria, then Seth, and last, Zane, my apparent doppelganger. But if it wasn't the rotten-faced man (I'm still refusing to say his name in case you haven't noticed) then what is the connection to me? Is there one? Does any of this have anything to do with me?

Maybe I haven't been sunshine and roses since we met. I mean, can you blame me? I was sitting at my dining room table being interviewed by that bitchy detective for hours while nursing a migraine. And since then, look at everything I've been through. But I promise, I'm usually a nice person to be around.

So why would someone be targeting me? Or people near me?

"I don't want to go over to Seth's house. It's late. And I'm sure his mom is a freaking mess right now. I, uh, should have gone over to see her after Seth disappeared, but I couldn't," I say to Max.

He nods.

"Yeah, it is pretty late. Maybe tomorrow?"

"Yeah, maybe," I mumble.

"Should we go back to Max's and check for more emails or comments on the podcast?" Nico suggests.

Emma uses the back of her hand and rubs her eyes, pushing her aquamarine hair out of her face. That's followed by a huge, clearly exaggerated yawn.

"Maybe we should go to my house and sleep," I suggest. "I mean, we are right here."

"But what about Max?" Nico asks.

"I'll be fine. I have my car. It's not like someone is going to run me off the road and abduct me between here and my house." His voice is strained, and he quickly turns it into an awkward chuckle to cover it up.

I shake my head. "No way, Max. You can sleep on my couch. The four of us don't go anywhere if we aren't together. Not until this shit's over."

"Right, okay. But my car is blocking the alley."

"We can pull it into our garage. There's room." I walk out of Gloria's room without giving it another look. I'm gonna have words for Gloria when we find her. Because we will find her. She needs to know that I'm kinda pissed at her. I mean, poetry? Art? Photography? She could have shown me this, even without talking to me.

We still could have been friends.

Gloria's parents are distracted when we go downstairs. We slip on our shoes and tiptoe out the back door—I throw Mr. Sanchez a quick wave and he waves back, then goes back to arguing with whoever is on the phone. I can't make out what he's saying, but it sounds intense.

The air outside is heavy with humidity. Like it wants to force me to crawl on my hands and knees. Nico, Emma, and I stand huddled in the alley while Max pulls his car into our garage. Dad used to keep an old truck in it, one we worked on together sometimes, until he sold it last year to pay for stuff at work. Maybe that's how he paid for part of the expansion at the gym. I guess I could have asked, but I was kinda pissed at him when I went to work on the truck one day and it was gone.

Gone, like so many things in my life.

My chest heaves as I pull the garage door down.

"Let's get inside quick, I feel like someone is watching us," Emma complains. We all run through the backyard and scare the crap out of my mom, who's in the kitchen pouring cat food for her devil cat Roscoe.

Chapter Twenty-Two

WHAT'S IN THESE THINGS?

After Mom stops scolding us for giving her a heart attack, she sends us all to bed. She doesn't care that Max is gonna be sleeping on the couch and grabs him the extra blankets and pillow from the hall closet. Emma and Nico take the guest room upstairs with the dusty floral bedspread. Dad's outside on the front porch, but from the look of his reflection through the window, he's fallen asleep on guard duty. His head is tilted to one side and resting on his hand.

"I'll worry about getting your father up to bed. He wanted to keep an eye on all the cars driving by to take pictures," Mom says. Then she kisses me on the head and tells me to get some rest. I trudge upstairs.

But as tired as my body is, I know I won't be able to sleep.

I'm afraid that the moment my eyes shut, I'll have nightmares. The rotten-faced man who haunts me is dead. But there's another monster out there, somewhere in the darkness. Are they plotting another attack? I lock my bedroom door, just in case, and turn my lights off, so anyone outside looking up can't see my shadow. I open the curtains just a sliver and look over the backyard. An eerie yellow glow radiates around each of the lamp posts along the alley, and every shadow could be the monster tiptoeing closer.

I back away with a shiver and curl into my black papasan chair and hold Mr. Puppy to my chest. The faint lavender smell is not enough to calm me. I'm overwhelmed with guilt. It's my fault the real one-eyed puppy didn't make it home with us all those years ago as we raced through the woods, trying to escape our cages. If I'd been faster, stronger, braver, I could have saved him. Maybe I could have saved all the puppies.

My cheeks sting with hot tears.

I need to find Gloria and tell her I'm sorry.

And I want to hold Seth in my arms and tell him just how much I love him. I don't know if he's like my forever person, but he is my right-now person, and I want him back. In one piece. Not with a missing eye, not with a missing limb, not with scars so deep he won't ever recover.

I laugh.

Who the hell am I kidding?

Of course he's going to have *scars so deep*. He's been abducted and held against his will! I pray he's somewhere close, but I don't know, where does a monster keep their prey? In a cage? In the woods? In a basement or an abandoned house?

The truth is, I don't feel any closer to figuring any of this out than I did the day Gloria was kidnapped. Sure, I know more about myself and what I went through when I was a kid, but has that really helped this situation? Is that giving me the clues I need to figure out who the hell took Seth and Gloria?

The answer is no.

"No." I take my puppy pillow away from my chest and look at him. "I don't know what I'm doing." I stare into his singular button eye. My heart speeds up. My adrenaline is seconds away from racing. Every thought in my mind is overwhelming and triggering. The air in my lungs is bitter and constricting... Don't say it. I already know! I'm about to have a full-blown panic attack. Sweat drips down my forehead and for a few seconds I see stars. Not outside in the night sky, but in my mind as I hover around the edge of consciousness.

I look at my phone. Midnight. It's probably too late to call Tammy. But I do it anyway, letting it ring, once, twice, three times. Just as I'm about to hang up, I hear a voice on the other end. "Hello? Grace? Are you safe? What's wrong?"

"No, I'm not fucking safe. I mean, yes. I'm at my parents' house. But I'm not mentally safe. I'm in a really bad place, Tammy. You're supposed to be my shrink, right? Well, you're doing a shitty job." I spew angry words, assaulting her through the phone.

She takes several heavy breaths, and it's really gross.

My face contorts and I contemplate hanging up.

"Do you need me to come over?" she finally offers.

"Ew, no, yuck. I just want you to talk me out of this panic attack. I don't want you to come to my house." Even though that's exactly what I need right now.

She growls, very un-doctor-like, if I do say so myself. "You've got two seconds Grace. I was sleeping and you're being a little b—"

I push the button to end the call before she can call me a bitch or brat or baby or whatever other B-word was on the tip of her tongue.

My heart racing shifts, from being on the verge of a panic attack to being ready to punch Tammy in the face. Seriously? Who does she think she is?

Grrrrr... now I'm the one growling.

I close my eyes and take a deep breath. I imagine shedding my skin and turning into a beast, someone big and strong with long razor-sharp claws. A beast who could rip anyone apart, tearing flesh from bone. Anyone like Tammy. Or like the rotten-faced man. Or the mysterious asshole who's stolen my friends.

Then I put my face into Mr. Puppy and scream as loud as I can.

The sound, muffled by his lumpy, compacted fluff, encapsulates years of my abuse. I scream, over and over and over, then I climb into my bed and sink into the darkness of dreamless sleep. When up is down and down is up and the only thing I know is I am in an alternate world and I am alone.

***

"Grace, it was so nice to have all you kids under one roof last night. I haven't slept that good in weeks," Mom says as she flips pancakes on the rectangular griddle. There are already two plates stacked ten cakes high on the table. But she's stress-cooking, and I'm not going to stop her. And I won't stab these ones to death either. My friends are having way too good of a time wrapping them around sausages and dunking in syrup before stuffing their faces for me to ruin it with another breakfast murder scene. Even though I'm steaming.

Max swallows his bite and opens his mouth to speak, saving me from saying anything, because I did NOT get a good night's sleep. Not after that call with Tammy and falling into the darkest depths of my mind. "Mrs. Everly, these are so good, do you do something special when you make them?"

"Well Max, the trick is, a dash of powdered sugar in the batter. Store-bought mix is kinda bland. But this makes them fluffier and sweeter." Mom smiles, thrilled someone finally asked her about her secret pancake mix.

He shoves another one in his mouth and nods. "Imma-tell-my-mom-ur-trick," he says with cheeks full of syrup-soggy pancake.

Nico and Emma giggle. "Storing those for winter?" Nico asks Max.

His face quickly turns a rosy shade of pink.

"You doing okay?" Mom flips the last pancake off the griddle and comes to put her arm around me. "Why don't you sit and eat some food with your friends. I'll, uh, leave you kids to it." She slinks out of the kitchen, and I sit down at the table.

"So, what are we doing today?" Emma asks. She pushes her empty plate forward and leans back with her hands over her belly. "Ugh, I ate too much."

I dish up some food and wait for Nico or Max to suggest our next move, focusing my energy on smearing butter and honey on my pancakes. When I look up, all eyes are on me. Oh great, they are hoping I'll come up with the plan. "No. Nope. You guys do it."

"What if we go to the library and talk to the librarian?" Nico suggests.

"What else do you think she's gonna tell us?" Max asks.

"Maybe she knows more about the man, like, maybe he has a brother or something," Nico says.

"Oh shit, yeah, I guess we never Googled him to learn more." Max pulls out his phone and starts searching for answers on his own. Guess the library is out.

"We could go see Dani and Sarah, find out more about the night Zane went missing." Emma shrugs. But the look on her face says she'd rather go shopping for a bra with her little brother than see Dani and Sarah. I don't blame her. That's the last thing I want to do today.

So, what is it I want to do today? If I could go anywhere or do anything, what would it be?

I'd still like to punch Tammy in the face for calling me a bitch last night. What was she even thinking? But it's been a long time since I've gone to her office. It gives me the creeps thinking about it. The long hallway past her office, leading into the big open "playroom" where I'd color pictures and build Legos. She always played with me when I was little, and I never had a clue she was performing therapy on me, getting me to forget and block out what happened to me.

But as my therapist, she must have notes from our sessions.

She might know a lot more about me than I remember about myself.

I can't believe Mom didn't think of this sooner!

"MOM!" I scream. My friends jump in their seats.

"Yes honey, what is it?" She's at my side in under three seconds, probably hovering near the doorway in the next room.

"I'm allowed to look at my medical records, right? I mean, they are mine. So can I go to my doctor's office and request them?" I ask. She looks confused, clearly this was the last thing she expected me to say.

"Well, I don't see why not. They are your records. What is it that you need? I can call the pediatrician's office and ask."

Does she really have no idea I mean Tammy?

Why would I want notes from my pediatrician?

I force myself not to roll my eyes. "Can you just write a note and sign it, that says you give your permission for me to have my medical records?" I stand up and head for the back door. Mom is quickly writing out my request on a sheet of notebook paper. She comes over and hands it to me, then pulls me into a hug. I let her hug me, my body melting into her arms.

"Stay together, the four of you. I'm not sure what this is all about but promise me you'll stick together." Mom doles out orders as my friends realize I'm serious and we are leaving right now. They don't ask any questions, they just walk out the back door, toward the garage where we left Max's car last night.

"Yes Mom, we promise," I agree.

"Okay, text me if you need anything. I'm going to the grocery store. Dad's already at the gym...you can always go there if..." But she doesn't finish what she's going to say.

"God, Mom, we'll be fine." I exit quickly after my friends, who are halfway across the yard. I'll fill them in once we get in the car. I fold up the note Mom wrote and shove it in my back pocket, it's just as backup in case Tammy wants to give me hell when I ask for my files.

Yesterday we thought we had to start at the beginning and that it meant going back to Gloria's house. Only now I realize, we have to go back to the very beginning...

Chapter Twenty-Three

ABANDONED LOT

"**S**o you think Tammy has information about what happened to you and Gloria in a file in her office?" Emma asks as we cruise down the oak-lined street. The Spanish moss waves gently in the breeze. "But why wouldn't she just tell you?"

"Because that's not how therapy works," I bark. Not that I really know how therapy works. I spent all those years 'helping' Tammy, never realizing I was her number-one client. Maybe if I had known I was a patient, I would have done things differently. My lips purse into an uncomfortable pout.

Max glances over at me. "You okay? Quite the face you've got there."

I flip the visor down and look at myself in the mirror. Just like I do when I'm trying to mimic Gloria's somber doll face. I start laughing as soon as I see the bitchy scowl.

"Girl, Max called you out!" Nico laughs.

Emma giggles and snorts, then makes eye contact with me in the mirror.

"Sorry, Emma. I didn't mean to snap at you." I unbuckle and turn myself around in the seat to look at my friends.

She smiles and shrugs. "It's okay. I'm used to it."

"You shouldn't have to be used to it. I should be a better friend!" I stick my hand out and she grabs on to it and squeezes. "I love you guys. I don't know what I'd do without you."

"Aw, we love you too," Emma says. "Right, Nico?"

"'Till death do us part." Nico winks.

"I hate to break up the wedding, but uh, Grace, I don't know where we are going," Max says. Oh shit, I was supposed to be navigating. I turn around and sit back into my seat, pulling the belt over and clicking it into place. I look around. Max has driven us along 3rd Street, past Tammy's office.

"Um, we passed her office, we'll have to turn around. It's in that little row of houses behind the empty lot."

"It's Saturday. Maybe we should go to her house?" Nico asks.

"Wait, it's Saturday? Man, my days are off!" I look at my phone to verify. Sure enough, it's Saturday. The last few weeks have been a vacuum of time and space. I don't want to go to Tammy's house and demand to look at my medical records. That feels invasive, going to her home. I'm not even sure I remember how to get there. It's been a long time.

"Um... Let's check her office first. She might work on Saturday, I don't know."

Max pulls into the Publix and whips his car around, making us all slip and slide and laugh and scream. He smirks, such a guy thing to do.

"Hang on!" he teases as he heads back in the direction of Tammy's office, weaving around cars like a maniac. When we arrive, there aren't any cars in the driveway or on the street.

"Park down the block, just in case." I point to a spot near some other cars.

We've only been driving for fifteen minutes, but we all stretch as if we've been stuck inside his car for hours on a long road trip to Atlanta. A long and wild ride, I might add.

"Why is her office in a neighborhood?" Max asks as we walk toward the office. "It looks like a regular house."

"Yeah, it was my grandma's old house. Well, her and her twin sister. Tammy's mom. When Grandma died, she left it to Tammy and she fixed it up and turned it into her office," I explain.

It's an older street with a big empty lot on one side and the other houses are junky. Only Tammy's office is nicely manicured and well taken care of. I look up and down the block. It's kinda creepy now that I look around, not someplace you want kids to go for trauma therapy. Let's be honest, this is not some place you want kids to be at all, right? Trauma therapy in a shitty neighborhood. Why don't you just pin a sign on their back that says, HI! MY NAME IS FUCKED-UP.

What?

We were all thinking it.

"You know, if we wanted to livestream a podcast episode, that empty lot would be perfect. It's super creepy," Nico says.

I look over at it; the grass is overgrown and brown. A row of half-dead oaks line the back, and there are rotted mounds of plume grass, lining a long-forgotten path to nowhere. Throw in the dumped trash covered in spiderwebs and you've got yourself a fun place to catch hepatitis. I'm surprised Tammy hasn't had the city over there to mow it all down.

"You know, it kinda looks like there was a house there, see in the middle?" Emma points and wags her finger around, drawing a house.

"Actually, it was an old church—from the 1920s," Max says and holds his phone up and shows us a black-and-white picture of an old brick church. Churches are a dime a dozen in our town. You know how in Seattle there is a Starbucks on every corner? Well, in places like Richmond Hill, there's a church on every corner.

"Big whoop, a church." I flip off the empty lot, just to prove how much I don't care.

"GRACE!" Nico and Emma both yell. Their parents still try to make them go to church. Snoozefest.

"Come on, we're here to see about my medical records, not eff around with that spooky lot. We can come back another time if you're so desperate." I march up the walkway and knock on the door. I don't expect anyone to answer. Clearly Tammy is not here, but it's worth a shot. I wait a few seconds before I knock again and ring the doorbell.

"TAMMY!" I scream.

Nico and Emma walk up behind me and just as I'm about to pound on the door one last time, something loud bangs from inside.

"What was that?" Nico hisses and she and Emma crouch behind me.

"Shhhhh!" I press my ear up against the door. I close my eyes and try and focus on the sounds behind the door. Someone is definitely in there. I can hear footsteps.

"Should you call Tammy? Maybe her phone will ring from inside and we can hear it," Emma suggests.

I slowly turn around, staring at her and Nico in their foolish position hiding behind me. It's actually a solid plan. Sometimes Emma really is the smartest one in our group. I pull my phone from my pocket and dial Tammy's number. It rings once, then twice, then three times before Tammy answers. There's music on in the background.

"What do you want Grace? I'm kinda busy at dance class," Tammy sounds out of breath, there's muffled scraping sounds and then a door slams shut. She must be walking out of class to speak to me privately. Great, she's going to yell at me for sure.

"I uh, wanted to say I'm—" I pause.

"If you're calling to apologize for last night, it's fine. I'm sorry too, I shouldn't have snapped. How about I come over after dance class and we can talk in person," she offers.

"NO!" I shout. I don't want her coming to my parents' house when I'm not there and finding out that I'm snooping around her office. "I mean, no, not today—I'm on my way to the mall with my friends. How about tomorrow?"

"Okay, sounds good. Have fun at the mall." She hangs up quickly.

"It's not Tammy inside," I tell Nico and Emma. "She's at some dance workout class or something."

"Well, if it's not Tammy, then who's inside her office?" Nico asks. Her eyes are gleaming, probably a combination of fear and excitement.

"Only one way to find out. Let's sneak around the back and see if we can see anything." I take two steps off the porch, when the sound of screeching tires gives me a jump scare. I look down the block, and at the end of the street there's a dark van racing away. I dunno where it came from, but it gives me the heebie-jeebies. Because you know, white windowless vans are synonymous with kidnappers. And it was a dark van that took Gloria.

"Uh, guys, I think you should come see this," Max shouts. He's standing in the middle of the empty lot, nearly lost in the overgrown mess.

I roll my eyes. Doesn't Max know we are on to something? We don't have time for whatever crap he's found. It's probably a dead racoon or something gross that only a guy would think trumped hearing noises in a house that is supposed to be empty.

But Emma and Nico are clearly interested, because they both go running down Tammy's walkway and cross the street toward Max.

Since I don't want to go behind the house by myself, I have no other option than to cross the street and see what Max has his panties in a twist over.

Except when I get there, I wish I'd gone around to the back of the house.

I wasn't prepared for what I was about to see.

Chapter Twenty-Four

THE SHRINE

"Should we call the police?" Nico asks.

"No." I take a picture, then another, and another, making sure to get different angles. Sweat drips around the edge of my hairline, catching in the soft baby hairs and sliding into my ear. It tickles and instinct makes me reach a hand up to wipe it away.

In the middle of the overgrown abandoned lot, where an old church once stood whose outline is peeking out of the tufts of dead grass, sits something truly terrifying. Emma was right when she used her finger to draw an outline—this place has the shape of a long-forgotten place of worship. The jagged rocky foundation is still visible under the mountains of weeds and junk.

But none of that matters. What matters is the stone and wood altar in the center.

"Grace, are you okay?" Emma pats my shoulder.

I ignore her and take more pictures.

If I look at it through the screen of my phone, it isn't so scary.

"This shit is messed up," Nico says. "I really think we should call the cops."

"I agree with Nico," Max says and rubs his hands over his face and shakes his head.

I let out a long, sorry-sounding sigh. "Fine. Call the cops." I pocket my phone and walk away from *The Shrine*. Yeah, I'm giving it a formal name. I mean, what else can you call pictures of Gloria, Seth, and Zane, surrounded by candles and flowers and trinkets, sitting at the base of the altar. Like who the hell is out here worshipping them, or mourning them, or doing some kind of deep southern magic (yeah, that's a thing, if you don't know, look it up online).

But the thing that has all of us freaked out the most, or at least I assume it's why my friends are cross-eyed, is there aren't just pictures of Gloria, Seth and Zane. Nope. That would be too easy. We could laugh it off as a religious zealot out here at the ruins of a church, praying for their souls or some idiots from our school pulling a prank or making a TikTok. No, the thing we are freaking out about are the pictures of us. Me, Emma, Nico, and even Max. Our faces are in little wooden frames sitting next to the others, with candles and beads and flowers around them. What the actual fuck.

***

"Grace, I have literally no idea why your pictures are out there. I've been begging the city for years to clean up that lot. Nothing but teenagers partying at night and vagrants sleeping during the day," Tammy says as she paces around the room. She pauses to look at me, pleading with her eyes for me to believe her. But, come on, it's pretty suspicious that it was right in front of her office.

How could she not know it was out there?

We are sitting four across on the red couch in the playroom, aka the active therapy room. As soon as the cops showed up, I called Mom, who called Tammy, who arrived within minutes all sweaty and in gym clothes. So, I guess she was telling the truth, she was at a dance class and not in the basement of her office doing something weird and creepy.

I'm still freaked out about the loud crashing sounds we heard earlier. Not to mention the creepy dark van that sped away right after.

I glare at her. "You should have called my dad to clean up that lot if the city wasn't gonna do it." I fold my arms over my chest and sink back into the couch. My friends are quiet. Which is unlike them. I glance over. Emma and Nico have their heads buried in their phones, texting each other, if I'm not mistaken.

Tammy won't let any of us leave and it's stressing me out.

She said it would be irresponsible not to have our parents pick us up. Even Max! And he has his own car parked right down the block.

An officer pops his head in, thankfully it's not one I've had contact with lately. "Ma'am, do you mind stepping outside to speak with us for a few minutes?" Tammy squeaks and darts out of the room.

As soon as the front door shuts, Max stands up and heads for the back door. His Vans silently stride over the wood floors. "This place gives me the ick. Let's get out of here."

Nico and Emma are right behind him. Not being as quiet, they thunder for the door.

I'm on my feet but heading the other way before I can change my mind. I don't want to be here when my parents arrive. I don't want to be in this house-turned-office for one second longer than I have to be. But I want my records.

No. I *need* my records.

"Grace, what are you doing?" Nico asks. I look over my shoulder and watch as Max and Emma slip out the sliding glass door. Nico is waiting for me and waving her hand. Her hair is messy and she urges with a flailing hand.

"Go. I'll meet you guys back at Max's place. I want my file."

I know I don't have long before Tammy comes back inside or my parents show up. But if I can just get that file, I'll be able to answer so many questions! My heart pounds in my ears with every step I take toward the bedroom that Tammy uses as her private office.

"Please don't be locked," I whisper as my hand clasps the metal doorknob. It turns in my sweaty grasp, and as I go in, I hear the front door open. "Shit." I slip in, close the door and flick the lock, but I'm sure Tammy has a key, so I grab one of the chairs in front of her big desk, and shove it under the knob to keep it from opening. I hope.

"Grace!" Mom's voice echoes and her footsteps pound down the hallway.

"Shit, shit, shit," I hiss. I've got to make this fast and get the hell out of here. The window behind the desk is my only escape route now.

"Tammy! The kids aren't here." Mom's voice sounds like it's right next to me, even though I know she's yelling from in the playroom.

The wooden drawers below the window are where Tammy keeps the patient files. I know, because I've seen her put them in there before. I fit my fingers in the hidden lip and tug, but the drawer doesn't come loose. Oh great. So *this* she locks? I pull harder and the entire cabinet shakes. I spin back to her desk and look around, frantic to find a key or a letter opener I might be able to pry the drawer open with. Her desk is cluttered with papers, and I push them around quietly until I spot something—a little seashell-shaped dish with a couple paper clips and BINGO! A set of small silver keys.

I grab the keys and as fast as I can, I unlock the drawer and slide it open. My fingers fly through the tabs on each file, thankfully they are in alphabetical order. But until I see my name, I'm not going to relax. The air in my lungs burns... *Davidson, Duke, Edwards...* come on, please, be here, ahhhh... *Everly.*

I rip the file from its place. Should have known it would be the thickest one.

Rattle.

Shake.

Knock.

"Why is this door locked?" Tammy asks. "Grace? Are you in there?" She's banging on the door, with closed fists. The noise sounds like a gunshot. Bang! Bang! Bang!

"Watch out Tammy, let me try. Grace, honey! It's Mom! Please, are you kids hiding in there? It's okay! Open up!"

I don't have time to think, I shove the drawer closed, stuff the file into the front of my pants, hoping it will stay put and then I crawl up on the cabinet. The window has a white flip switch. I flick it then lift the window up as fast as I can. I duck my head through, banging the crown of my scalp, damn it! That's gonna leave a mark.

I manage to get out of the opening and jump through the window, landing on the soft grass outside, in a crouching position like some cartoon ninja. I feel at my waist, the file is still there. I don't look back to see if Tammy has gotten into her office. I start running, ducking behind bushes and trees, hoping not to get caught by the police out front. Car tires squeal in the distance and I sure hope that's my friends getting the freak out of here.

Chapter Twenty-Five

THE FILE

Did you know it's like five miles if you drive from Tammy's office to Max's house, but if you cut through neighborhoods and alleys it's only three miles? That would take an average person about an hour to walk. But not me. Remember, I like to walk, and Gloria has long legs, so I am used to walking fast.

I manage to reach Max's house in about thirty minutes. Okay, maybe I ran here instead of walking. Can you blame me? Every noise had me in a cold sweat, thinking I was being followed, by cops, my parents, Tammy, the shrine builder, a kidnapper—the list of people stressing me out is growing longer by the second.

"Grace!" Nico shrieks as soon as I open the shed door in Max's backyard. Her black hair is still wild and her eyes look even wilder. Like she's some feral cat. I'm about to say as much when she and Emma leap at me, nearly knocking me to the ground. My legs are a little rubbery from all the running.

"Whoa," I exclaim as they pull me in and slam the door shut.

"We wanted to wait for you, but Max said it was safer to come back here," Emma says, nervously bouncing from foot to foot like she does before her soccer games.

"You guys did the right thing." I'm grateful Max brought them back here. If they'd waited for me, they would have been caught for sure.

"Our parents are blowing up our phones," Nico says, as her phone buzzes. She looks at it and rolls her eyes. "Obviously I'm not kidnapped, Mom, stop texting me," she yells at the screen.

"We have to get to the bottom of this now. We can't live like this." I lift up my shirt. Max quickly averts his eyes and I start laughing, throaty and dry. "I'm not flashing you, big dork. I have the file." I pull it from its spot wedged in my pants and drop it on the coffee table in front of the couch. It makes a slapping sound, and I finally have a chance to see how thick it really is.

"Ohhhh." Max blushes and throws his head back, shaking his hair from his eyes.

I slump on the couch, Emma and Nico sit on either side of me, and we stare at the fat manila folder. I lean forward to lift up the cover, then I pause. "This feels like a Red Bull and K-pop moment."

"Girl, you read my mind." Nico turns on music from her phone.

"Catch!" Max grabs three sugar-free Red Bulls from the fridge and tosses them one at a time to Emma. She passes them to us while Max drags a camp chair to the coffee table so he can get a closer look at the file with us.

"You really want to see what's in that thing? Once you see it, you can never erase it from your mind," Nico warns and narrows her eyes.

"Yeah, I'm counting on it. I want my memories back. It was wrong for my parents and Tammy to erase them from me—even if they thought it was to protect me." I chug half the energy drink and wipe my lips on my sleeve all dramatically.

Emma giggles, I can sense a nervous edge to her laughter. "I'm kinda nervous," she admits.

"Me too." I take her hand and squeeze it. "But if there's clues in here that will help us find out what happened to Gloria and Seth, we have to face it. Right?" I suck in a deep breath. I reach my hand out, it's trembling, and the moment it touches the folder, I jerk it back. Like a reflex when you touch something hot and burn your fingers. Yeah, I know, totally ridiculous. I literally just had the file in my pants for thirty minutes, I know it's not hot lava.

"We'll do it together." Nico sees me struggling and rips the Band-Aid off by flipping the folder open, exposing an intake cover sheet with a picture of me when I was four years old. "There's a lot in here. Let's divide and conquer. We can each take a stack, skim it for clues, and if anything looks suspicious, put it in a pile here."

Thank God for Nico! Because I was having serious second thoughts. I mean, I don't want to relive every stupid "this isn't ther-apy" therapy session I spent with Tammy. I just want to know the big things. Like, did I tell her anything that might lead us to who has my best friend and boyfriend? Yeah, yeah, and Zane too.

Nico scoops up the papers, dividing them into four equal stacks and hands them out to each of us. I lean back on the couch, tuning out the world around me, carried away by the handwritten words on each page. Tammy's language is clinical and precise, devoid of any real emotion, and her penmanship looks like Arial typeset.

June 18

Session #3

Today, Grace opened up about her time in captivity. She said she was brave. When I asked her to explain what that meant, she looked at me puzzled. Her eyes narrowed and she asked me if I was brave. When I responded yes, I was brave, she laughed at me and shook her head. Then she refused to speak the remainder of the session. She is more difficult than I thought she would be.

June 19

Session #4

Grace asked for a snack, then took a nap on the floor.

June 20

Session #5

Grace spent the entire session coloring pictures of a one-eyed dog. When I asked her to talk about the dog, she said its name was Mr. Puppy and he was the reason she and Gloria were able to escape. NOTE - Explore Mr. Puppy in future sessions.

I flip through, skipping around to find something more interesting.

July 15

Session #25

Grace is exhibiting compulsive behaviors, lining the toys and crayons up perfectly. Parental interviews confirm the same behavior at home. Excessive hair brushing, teeth brushing, handwashing.

August 23

Session #50

Grace still refuses to speak to me after I asked her if she enjoyed being in the cage with Gloria.

What a bitch! Why would she ask me that? I quickly thumb through the rest of the stack; I can't stand to read each one of these notes. They aren't helpful, and I'm glad I was more difficult than Tammy imagined I would be. Way to go little Grace! Giving Tammy the cold shoulder when she asked dumbass questions. I shake my head and a chuckle escapes my lips. I glance over to my friends to see if any of them find my childhood behavior as funny as I do.

Emma wipes a tear from her eye.

And Nico has pulled her knees up to her chest and her face is twisted with horror, like she's eating a lemon.

Max sets his papers down and stands up, huffing with disgust, then goes over to the computer. He puts his headphones on—clearly, he doesn't want to talk about whatever it is he read in my file.

Yikes!

Does it really get that bad?

I wonder what could possibly have all my friends so freaked out.

Did I miss something in my pages? I thumb through them again. I have the first year of notes, as far as I can tell, and it's a pretty boring daily account of my early sessions with Tammy. A lot of the same, where she starts making some progress, then asks me something inappropriate and I ignore her for several weeks.

"My pages are crap." I set them down on the table. "Emma, why are you crying? It can't be that bad, right?"

Emma puts her pages down and gives me a huge hug. She sobs into my shoulder. "Oh Grace! Tammy was so mean to you. She was using some kind of hypnotherapy, she wanted to break you, not help you!"

Nico slams her pages down. "Same in mine. Tammy is a... I'm gonna say it, y'all know I hate the word, but I'm gonna say it! Tammy is a bitch. She wasn't helping you, she was experimenting on you. Gloria was in treatment with her too, but not for long, sounds like her dad freaked out and pulled her in the middle of a session."

"What? Really?" Now that's something I didn't know. She never told me she was in treatment with Tammy—oh right, she wasn't speaking to me. Duhhhhh!

"She only mentions Gloria because she was concerned that you saw her leaving with her dad and crying and it might trigger your memories."

Nico takes her phone and searches something online. "Look what this says: *Patients who have gone through trauma are more susceptible to hypnosis.*" She holds her phone out for me to read something. Then she pulls it back and does some more online sleuthing.

I know I should feel something about this.

Shocked.

Angry.

Surprised.

But I feel numb. I'd already known that Tammy was using some mind-erasing techniques to make me forget what happened while Gloria and I were abducted. That's something I'll have to sort through for the rest of my life. What I wanted to find out, by looking in my file, was if I said something back then that we might use to figure out where our friends are now. Unfortunately, it looks like it's another dead end.

I collect the papers and shove them back into the file.

Letting out a long sigh, I realize I fucked this up. "I'm sorry guys, I was convinced there would be something in there that would open another door. But it was just a waste of time. We are right back where we started. Again!"

Ugh! This is so frustrating. It's been weeks.

That's when Max pulls his headphones down. "It's not all been a waste of time. I found something."

"I didn't think you were listening." I stand up and walk over to stand behind him, looking over his shoulder at his computer screen. He's got the Richmond Hill Library page pulled up. "I don't know why I didn't check before, but that email we got, from the librarian—she's not listed as one of the staff at the library."

"Maybe she's new." I shrug.

"Or maybe she doesn't work at the library at all," he says.

I have no idea where he's going with this.

"So what," Nico says. Echoing my thoughts exactly. So what. Someone pretended to be a librarian to send us a tip about the rotten-faced man being dead. Maybe they were trying to protect their identity. Although that's kind of a weird way to protect your identity. Posing as a librarian?

"The email said her name was Ms. Kemper. But look, it isn't from a city email address—it's a generic email," he explains. "I should have double-checked. But I was distracted by the article."

"Okay, so some rando pretended to be a librarian to send us the article. Stranger things have happened." But I have a feeling it goes deeper and that Max is about to tell us more.

"When I was looking at the pages in your file, Grace, I came across some entries written by Tammy's intern. A recent college grad named Lizzie Kemper. Do you remember her?" Max asks.

Lizzie Kemper?

Why does that name sound so familiar?

A pain erupts behind my left eye, a memory wants to escape, and I'm going to either pass out—my knees are trembling and my mouth fills with saliva—or I'm going to have the worst migraine on the planet. I shake my head back and forth and will myself not to black out. I close my eyes and shove my thumb into the fleshy part of my eyelid, pushing down hard and massaging, hoping the pain will subside.

"Grace, are you okay?" Emma asks.

"Bitch, do not pass out. Stay with us," Nico says and puts her arm around me. "Tell us about Lizzie Kemper. Who is she? What did she do to you?"

I open my mouth to say I don't know who the hell she is, but instead, when I speak, the words on my tongue begin to tell a story. One I didn't remember until today.

***

"Grace! Wait up!" Lizzie yells at me as I dart across the parking lot. But I'm excited to get to the library. It's my new favorite thing about going to therapy. Tammy is too busy with her real patients to need me to help her anymore, but she told me Mommy still needs this time alone every day, so we just pretend I'm still helping. But in reality, she has her new intern Lizzie drive me in her car to the library to read books. I don't mind. I love the way the library smells, all the ink and paper. Plus, Mrs. Hoffstead, the librarian, has a candle she burns behind the desk that smells like pumpkin pie.

Lizzie glares at Mrs. Hoffstead every time we come in and she sees the candle.

"It's disrespectful to have an open flame in this place," Lizzie whispers to me. "If I was the librarian, I would never do that."

But it's cozy and comfy, and I like the smell of pumpkin pie.

"Ugh, Lizzie, you say that every time we come here, don't you get bored of saying the same thing every single day?" I ask.

"No," she hisses. She looks at me and softens, then uses her hands to smooth down my hair, which must be wild, because she's smoothing it a lot. Like she's petting a dog. "I tried to get a job here you know, but Mrs. Hoffstead said she didn't need any help."

Then she wanders off to her section of the library. She lets me go to the kids' section on my own because it isn't that far, and I quickly find the latest book I was reading, take it from the shelf and plunk down in a beanbag chair. I flip to where I left off and secretly folded the corner, and begin to devour the words on the page, a smile spreading over my face. It's just getting to the good part when—

"No, stop it, don't touch me, Eustis!" Lizzie yells.

"Get yer ass out of that chair. Always got your ugly pig nose stuck in a book," a man yells. His voice sounds terrifyingly familiar and coaxes fear from the very depths of my soul. My body clenches in response. I feel something hot and wet between my legs. Tears are streaming down my face and I know I just peed my pants.

"NO!" Lizzie's voice sounds twice as loud in the quiet of the library.

"But Ma needs you back at the farm, you selfish little bitch. She got a bad back and can't help me load the containers no more," the man hollers.

"I ain't goin back to that dump, so fuck off," Lizzie screams.

I can't see what's happening behind the shelves of books. But I don't need to see it to know the sound of chairs toppling and grown-ups fighting.

"Grace, come with me right now, keep your head down," Mrs. Hoffstead whispers. She crouches in front of me and pries the book from my rigid hands.

"I can't, I had an accident," I whimper.

"It's okay baby, I'll clean it up," she says. And even though she looks like a grandma, she has enough strength to scoop me up, pissy pants and all, and carries me from the kids' section of the library–through a doorway into the back part of the library, a place I've never been before. She carries me down some steps, into the library basement. I'm disoriented, but I'm not scared with Mrs. Hoffstead. She wouldn't hurt me—that much I know.

"I have to call the police, you stay hidden behind this box of books. I'll come back when it's all clear upstairs."

I grab her hand, and don't let go. "Please, don't leave me here."

"I have to help Lizzie, her brother isn't a very nice man."

"I don't want him to hurt you," I cry. I don't know what's going on, why is Lizzie's brother at the library? And why did his voice sound so familiar? My body aches from a pain I don't know how to explain. A sharp sting shoots up from my feet to my head and I lean over and throw up.

"It's okay Grace, I won't leave you. I'll see if I can get a signal down here," Mrs. Hoffstead says. She pulls her cell phone from her back pocket and holds it up in the air.

I curl up on the floor behind the box of books and close my eyes.

I must fall asleep, because when I wake up, I'm at home in my own bed. It's dark outside the windows—my Mr. Puppy pillow is next to me and I clutch him to my chest.

"Mommy!" I scream. "Daddy!"

My parents come rushing into my room, wide-eyed, but still half asleep. "Grace, are you okay, what's wrong?" Mommy asks.

Daddy scoops me up into his arms and holds me tight.

"What happened to Lizzie? Is she okay?" I ask. I don't remember leaving the library, and I hope Lizzie didn't get hurt by that man.

"Shhhh... you're just having bad dreams." Mommy pets my head.

"No, today, at the library—there was a man, he was fighting with Lizzie," I insist.

"Honey, we didn't go to the library today. You were helping Tammy, remember, you stayed and played with her for a few hours today," Mommy says. "Let's get you tucked back in. Mark, put her down please."

"But, Leanne, she's scared," Daddy says. He doesn't want to put me down, I know because he holds on tighter. "Are we sure these sessions are really helping? I swear, she comes home more traumatized than—"

"Mark, be quiet. Put her down and come to bed. Now." Mommy is angry and points at the door. Daddy sets me back on my bed, pulls the covers up, and gives me a kiss on the forehead.

"Sleep tight little bug," he whispers.

Mommy is frustrated and leaves without saying she loves me, even though I know she does. But now she's mad at Daddy and when she's mad at him she isn't much fun.

I hold on to Mr. Puppy, sucking in a deep breath of his lavender scent. "It felt pretty real," I tell him. Because it did. It didn't feel like a dream, today at the library. It felt like I was really there and really peed my pants.

Tomorrow I'm going to ask Lizzie about it and about that man.

But there wasn't a tomorrow.

Lizzie stopped being Tammy's intern. We can't talk about Lizzie. Tammy says Lizzie isn't real. She's just someone in my dreams.

Chapter Twenty-Six

You're One of Us

"Holy shit Grace, you remembered all of that right now?" Emma asks. Her eyes are red and bugged out from the tears that keep falling.

"Ah, Emma, don't cry!" I exclaim. My almost-migraine has gone away. Once the memory of Lizzie at the library came out of my mouth, I felt a million times better. Kinda like when you have a stomachache and walk around moaning, but as soon as you puke, you're like hell yeah what's for dinner.

"How can I not cry! That was horrible." She folds her arms over her chest.

"Horrible, but incredibly helpful," Max says. "Grace, do you know what you just did? You unlocked this thing." He spins around in his chair and starts searching and typing on his computer.

He's right. We have actual information we can go off of to figure out where Gloria, Seth, and Zane are. The rotten-faced man might be dead, but his sister Lizzie is still out there.

"So, Ms. Kemper, you lying bitch, you're not a librarian, you're a former intern who helped your brother kidnap little girls." Nico punches her fist into her hand.

"Well, we don't know that she was helping him." I come to Lizzie's defense. I don't know why, but she doesn't feel like the bad guy. I didn't gag when I remembered her.

"Do you really think your parents didn't know Tammy had an intern that took you to the library?" Emma asks.

"I don't think my parents knew anything that was happening at Tammy's." There are so many screwed-up layers to this thing. I'll probably spend years in *real therapy* unraveling all of it someday, but for now, all I want to do is find Gloria and Seth.

"Do you think Lizzie sent that email pretending to be a librarian to unlock a memory for you?" Max asks.

"No way! She's the kidnapper!" Nico answers for me.

"But why would Lizzie kidnap them?" I ask. "The rotten-faced man is dead. We only know that because she sent the email with the news article. If she was involved, why even send us that message?"

"Maybe she was trying to throw you off the case. Her message was to tell us that the rotten-faced man was dead," Max says. "So you'd stop looking in that direction. The podcast was about what happened to you and Gloria as kids. Maybe she thought it was only a matter of time before you remembered *her*, since you remembered *him*."

I rub my hands over my face.

Emma sniffles. "I think Nico and Max are right. I think it's Lizzie. We have to find her."

"What if we email her back, say that we know it's her and we are getting the police involved to nail her ass," Nico offers.

"But then she might kill them!" Emma shrieks.

Max nods his head. "She listens to our podcast. I mean, uh, she listens to *your* podcast." He pauses and shades his eyes with his hair. "What if *we*, shit, I mean *you*, do another episode and set a trap to lure her out."

"Max. You can say 'we.' Because as far as I'm concerned, you are part of *What's in the Woods?* from now until the end of time," I say with a smile.

"Yes! Max you are one of us now," Emma shouts, finally a smile on her face and a twinkle in her eyes.

Nico remains quiet, and we all stare at her, waiting for her to agree Max can be part of the podcast crew. She snorts once, then crouches down and puts her hands in front of her like claws, curls her lips, and snarls like a beast. "But, Max, if you want to join us, that means we have to turn you. You'll be a weirdo like us forever. Ahhhoooooo!" She lifts her head and howls.

Max grins, then jumps from his chair, throws his head back and howls.

"Oh, so is this a thing now? Werewolves?" I ask and laugh.

"Ahoooooo!" Emma howls.

My friends are the best, even if we are a bunch of weirdo-nerds. I tilt my head back and let out the loudest wolf cry I can. We all laugh and fall onto the couch in a pile of legs and arms and giggles.

It takes some time before we settle down. I guess we needed a release, you know, something like a howl session to burn up some of this nervous, anxious, angry energy about what's been happening to us and our friends.

"Let's do it. Let's set a trap for Lizzie with a new podcast episode. But it's gotta be something she'll never expect. Something believable, but also a little ridiculous," I announce.

"Ridiculous?" Max asks.

"Yeah—" I pause to think and close my eyes, blocking the noise of my friends chattering out of my mind. I think of the ocean, the waves crashing, like white noise. A smile slides over my face—I love the beach, the ocean, I can't wait to go there again, with Gloria and Seth.

I let out a long sigh.

The last time I was sitting on the beach at Tybee Island, I was with Dad, after Seth was kidnapped. My mind was such a mess that day, shit, I almost drowned! I even imagined Seth was trapped inside one of those big shipping containers, being taken away from me forever. And then a lightbulb goes off.

"Guys, I have an idea…"

Within minutes, we are sitting around the table, with paper, pens, about to have a script-writing session for our next episode. And I have a feeling this will be our most important episode ever.

Chapter Twenty-Seven

LURING OUT A FAKE

ME: *Hey all you monster hunters. Welcome back to another episode of—*

NICO, EMMA & ME (All together): *What's in the Woods?*

Max plays that creepy music sequence he put together for our last episode.

EMMA (laughing): *Let's all give a big round of applause to our newest What's in the Woods? member, Max!*

NICO, EMMA & ME (All together, clapping): *Ahhhoooooo!*

MAX: *Thanks guys. I'll mostly be behind the scenes, you know, for the music and editing and stuff. But I'm happy to be here, especially for this hair-raising episode.*

NICO (leans into her microphone): *Ooooh, Max, you have me intrigued! What's got your neck prickling?*

MAX (somber, lips almost touching microphone): *We have some new information about what happened to Grace and Gloria. If you remember, last time, Grace told the true-crime story of her and her neighbor Gloria's childhood abduction.*

NICO: *How could we forget? I've had nightmares about it. But what you're saying is there's more to Grace and Gloria's story?*

MAX: *Yep, and who better to tell us the story than Grace herself.*

ME: *Thanks for that introduction guys. So, during our last episode, I told you about how I'd started remembering the kidnapping Gloria and I went through when we were kids.*

EMMA: *Yes, you did, and it was really scary!*

ME: *Sorry, Emma. I didn't mean to scare you, but it was pretty screwed up, and what was even worse is that we didn't know who the kidnapper was. But we received a tip that led us to the man who'd kidnapped me and Gloria... And to all of our surprise, he's dead.*

NICO, EMMA & MAX (Gasping)

ME: *Yep, that asshole is dead. Oops. Beep that one out Max.*

MAX (with a chuckle): *You got it.*

ME: *According to a police report and news article, the rotten-faced man died in a single-vehicle accident years ago. We'll post a link after the episode is over for all our listeners to see the true identity of the man who kidnapped me and Gloria.*

EMMA: *But if he's dead, what happened to Gloria, Seth, and Zane?*

ME: *That's a good question, Emma. I'm not entirely sure, but we did receive another tip from the same person.*

Max holds his finger up, for a dramatic pause, and plays a new creepy music sequence he was working on while we put the script together for the episode.

ME (taking a deep breath to lay the trap): *The librarian, oops, edit that out Max. I mean, the anonymous tip said, our friends are being held in some old shipping containers in the woods on the southside of Fort McAllister. Waiting as bait to lure out the headless ghost.*

EMMA (gasping): *Wait...like the story we told on our first episode? Where a headless Civil War ghost marches lost people into the woods at night and steals their souls to pay the toll to get to heaven? That Fort McAllister?*

ME: *That's the place. But the police are never going to help us if we say ghosts are involved.*

NICO: *The police are never going to help us anyway. Ghosts or not. But Grace, I'm confused... What exactly did this tip say?*

ME: *It said they saw a big, dark figure taking our friends into the woods in the direction of the old shipping containers. And since they were right about the rotten-faced man being dead, I have to believe they are right about this. So tonight, we are going to find our friends and uncover what's in the woods, once and for all.*

Max waves his hand, signaling the episode is done recording. "And we're done. Great job guys. I'll have it posted in about ten minutes—after editing out the librarian callout. Should I edit out the asshole?"

"No! Leave it in. That makes it more believable." I lean back in my chair and flex my hands, cracking each knuckle. "Let's just hope Lizzie takes the bait and meets us out there in the woods. She can't overpower all three of us."

"Unless she has a gun." Nico holds her fingers like a gun and pulls the trigger, making a pop sound with her freshly glossed lips.

"Nicooooo, that's not funny!" Emma looks around nervously, her aqua hair swishing side to side. "I don't want to get shot!"

"Relax Emma, Lizzie isn't going to shoot anyone. She's not a killer. I mean, if she was, wouldn't she have killed her disgusting brother?" I stand up and pace around.

"Well, she ain't right in the head. We should be prepared for anything. If the rotten-faced man really was her older brother, some sick shit was going on in their house. We have no idea what we are up against," Nico says.

I know she's right. We have no idea what we are getting into. There are so many variables. Maybe she won't listen to the podcast. Maybe she won't go into the woods to meet us. Maybe she is a killer and our friends are dead.

The thoughts swirl around making loud screaming noises in my head, like chunks of jagged ice in a blender.

"There's only one thing to do now." I put my hands on my hips. Nico nods, Emma purses her lips and Max looks kind of confused, unsure of what I might say next. "Now we prepare for a war. We need black clothes, flashlights, rope, and my punching gloves."

Chapter Twenty-Eight

Two Options

It took a lot longer to convince our parents that we needed another sleepover. What, after the cops showed up at Tammy's this morning and we all ditched to go back to Max's house and record the podcast. Which, by the way, has had a record number of listens. It's up to 647!

Let's just hope one of those is Lizzie.

After I explained to Mom that I was not in Tammy's private office (what proof does she really have?) and that my friends were just spooked because of that shrine thing so we had to get out of there... Well, Mom (and her bottle of wine) decided that, *YES*, it must have been pretty scary. And she can't really blame us for wanting to get away from Tammy and the drama.

"Are you sure you want to leave again and spend the night at Emma's house? I feel like you're never home anymore." Mom's apron is tied around her waist in a big saggy front bow. Her hair is disheveled and her shoulders are slumped forward, like she's half-asleep.

"Yes, Mom. School is starting on Monday, and I really don't want to be home alone tonight," I say. I'm shoving some clothes into my backpack to take to Emma's house.

"You're not alone! You have me and Dad!" She sounds hurt.

"Mom, I know that. But, after what happened earlier, and then, you know, Dad told me you and Tammy got a little heated—you probably want to take a bath and just relax." I'm still in shock over that. Dad said Mom put her hands on Tammy, like shoved her, when she accused me of stealing. So what if it's true? I mean, I took my own file. Technically that's not stealing. It's MY FILE. My personal information. Who the hell is Tammy to keep it from me?

Mom lets out a long sigh. "Well, as long as you're with your friends, I know you'll be safe. Just promise you won't stay up too late and you won't go anywhere alone or leave Emma's house."

"I promise I won't. Just popcorn, movies, and karaoke. You know us." So maybe that's a big fat lie. What else am I going to say? Sorry, we aren't staying at Emma's house, we are really going hunting for potential kidnappers in the woods outside of town in the middle of the night. A place where ghosts lurk in the shadows.

Mom narrows her eyes at me for a second, then smiles. "Good, good. I love hearing that you're trying to get past this. I was just telling your dad, we have all got to get back to living our normal lives." And just like that, I realize Mom, and probably everyone else in town, has decided that Gloria, Seth, and Zane are missing forever. I cannot believe she just said she wants me to get back to my normal life.

How can I get back to my normal fucking life?

My boyfriend is missing!

My neighbor, who I only recently discovered is probably my best friend and the person I've told more secrets to than anyone, is missing!

And what would life at school be like without my archnemesis Zane, who is also still missing!

I can't let Mom see how annoyed I am by what she just said or she might start second-guessing me.

Buzzzzzz.

I check my phone. My friends are here to pick me up.

"Gotta go. They are here to pick me up. Love you." I slip my backpack on and lean in to give Mom a hug goodbye.

"I wish you'd wear more color. This black really washes you out," she says as she's squeezing me.

I groan. God, she's so annoying.

***

I slam the car door and Max slowly pulls out of the driveway. The headlight beams bounce around, reflecting light and casting strange tall shadows on the mailbox and trees. Thank God there's not a line of cars on our road taking pictures of my house. That was ridiculous and totally uncalled for.

"Okay Grace, we were wondering, do you think we should take some backup with us? You know, like in case Lizzie shows up with the actual kidnappers?" Nico asks.

"Yeah, maybe Zane's friends want to be there." Emma's voice cracks with her suggestion. "It'll be less scary with more people, right?"

Great. My friends are getting cold feet.

"Max, can you drive to the gym? I need to get my boxing gloves from my locker," I ask before addressing this new plot twist—my friends backing out on our perfectly devised plan. Since when are they actually frightened by what's in the woods? "Emma, do you really think Sarah and Dani would be any help? Look, if you don't want to do this, you don't have to. But I'm going out there tonight, to try and catch Lizzie. I'm going to tie her to a tree and beat the shit out of her until she tells me what happened to Seth and Gloria."

"Grace!" Emma shrieks.

"What? Her brother held me and Gloria in a cage for weeks. She had to know it was me, that's why she was interning with Tammy. She wanted to be around me."

"You said you were going to pretend to punch her, not really punch her," Emma reminds me.

"Yeah, yeah, tomato, toe-mahhh-toe. Maybe I won't put my fists on her face. But I'm totally willing to, and that is what counts. Lizzie is evil, she deserves whatever I dish out." Until that moment, I didn't really think of Lizzie as the bad guy, since I'd suppressed the memories of her along with everything else in my fucked-up mind.

Let's be honest here!

There's no other reason for her to be involved—for her to know Tammy or to take me to the library as a kid—if it wasn't to try and steal me again. To finish the work her brother started.

Right?

It's a little after nine p.m. when we arrive at Fort McAllister. There are all kinds of places to park on the side of the road, where trailheads start at various points in the massive, wooded landscape. I remember coming here a lot as a kid. Just about every teacher I had in elementary would bring us here on one, even two field trips. It was more so they could get out of the classroom for a day, letting us kids run around to blow off steam, than to teach us the history.

Thankfully, because all four of us have been here more times than we can count, it doesn't feel as scary as going into the dark woods at night should feel. "Not so bad, right? Just like when we'd come here in school," I say, hoping my friends agree. I sling my boxing gloves by their tied strings around my neck, that way I don't have to carry them while we walk.

"Yeah, not too bad. Do any of you remember which way to those old shipping containers?" Max asks. He pops open the trunk of his car and gets out a flashlight, passing it to Nico. Then he hands a yellow plastic LED lantern to Emma before putting a coil of rope over his chest and shoulder. I'm impressed. It's like he's done this before, gone hunting at night. But there's no time to ask about his past as a hunter, we really need to start moving and keep our voices down as we approach the spot anyway.

Max takes the lead, while Nico, Emma, and I fall into a single-file line behind him and begin the dirt path trek into the woods. I know it's not going to be very difficult, since the trail is wide and packed down from the thousands of school children and tourists. But I also know to be careful of the stray pine needles that jump up and stab your shins. Take it from me, that shit hurts.

We walk for a long time in silence. Every shadow looks like Slenderman. The tall skinny trees are the perfect hiding spot for him to lurk behind waiting to snatch one of us when we aren't paying attention. Not that I'm scared of Slenderman. Or Skinwalkers or Demogorgons or any other imaginary boogeymen for that matter.

There is only one thing that scares me.

And that's not finding my friends, or worse, *finding them dead.*

I instinctively sniff the humid evening air, searching for the smell of rotting flesh. I mean, if I was gonna dispose of a dead body, out here would be a good place—the saw palmetto bushes are thick, the pine needles fall incessantly, and the southern air makes the vegetation decompose quickly. Mosquitoes buzz around my ears, and I smack at them, wishing I'd brought bug spray. The venom from several bites is seeping into my face, and I dunno if it's that or the adrenaline high I've been on for weeks, but I'm starting to get dizzy.

"Grace." Emma shakes my shoulder, snapping me out of the daze I've succumbed to.

"Huh?" I drawl.

"Max said we have to cut off the trail if we want to set the trap. Look, there are the old shipping containers," she says.

I blink a few times, clearing my head. Gazing out across the field, where Emma is pointing. There's some construction equipment littered around the containers. From what I remember, the last time I was on a school tour out here, they were supposed to be building a new outdoor pavilion with picnic tables and a bathroom. But like much of the south, things move slowly, and projects get forgotten, as evidenced by the long weeds surrounding everything.

I really hope we didn't come out here for no reason and that Lizzie shows up to confront us. The more I think about our plan, the more I see all the plot holes in it. But I can't worry about that now, I just have to set up with my friends and wait.

A twig snaps somewhere in the distance, and goosebumps ripple up my spine. There are plenty of critters out here in the woods, probably things we should be more afraid of than Lizzie. Gators and bobcats and even black bears are known to roam these parts.

"We can hide here," Max says. He's standing behind a rusted bucket from a loader a little ways off from the containers that gives us a good view of where the trailhead opens up. He removes his rope, then turns off the lantern, plunging us into darkness.

"Do we have to turn off the lantern?" Nico asks.

"It will give our location away if we don't," Max says. "Look, those clouds are clearing, the moon will give us enough light in a few minutes."

Sure enough, we stand there waiting quietly—the seconds feel like hours, but eventually the clouds part and the moonlight drifts into the clearing, giving us enough light to see. My eyes relax, not straining so much. I'm scanning all around, looking for a flashlight or anything that might alert us that Lizzie is approaching.

Another stick cracks, this time much closer. I spin around.

"Did you hear that?" I hiss.

Emma grabs onto my arm. "Hear what?" she asks.

I squint. It's hard to see very deep into the woods, the moonlight doesn't reach the forest floor, and the underbrush is thick. Anything could be hiding out there. Suddenly this plan feels less and less like a good idea, and more and more like how we all become the next victims of an abduction.

"Uh guys, what's that?" Nico asks. Emma and I spin back around and look at what Nico is pointing at. There is a bluish bobbing light way off beyond the clearing, on the other side of the shipping containers. It's on the opposite side of the trailhead in the woods. That's strange. How would someone be coming from that direction? There's nothing out there except more woods, and the Ogeechee River.

Every fiber in my body tenses. My breathing quickens and my heart pounds in my ears, making it hard to hear.

"It's gonna be okay," Max says in a throaty whisper, not to me specifically, but to all of us. Even himself.

We huddle together, peeking out from behind the thick rusted metal bucket, waiting to see if that blue light is coming from Lizzie or someone else.

"Boo." A hand clamps hard on my shoulder from behind and I spin and throw a punch, connecting my bare knuckles with something soft, feeling it crunch under the weight of my fist.

"Ouch, Grace!" Dani's hands instinctively go up to her face. "You broke my nose, bitch!"

"Oh, shit," Nico exclaims.

Max quickly flips on the lantern.

"Dani, are you okay?" Sarah asks, trying to get a look at her friend's face. Dani is sniffling and whimpering.

"Well, what the fuck did you think would happen?" I demand. "Sneaking up on us like that?"

Emma elbows me.

"Sorry, Dani. I didn't mean to break your nose. Let me look," I offer to help, extending a hand.

"Get away from me." Dani flinches.

Max steps in. "Here, let me take a look. I see broken noses a lot at the gym." He hands the lantern to Sarah. "Hold this so I can see. Nico, can you grab something to stop the bleeding. I think there's a rag in my backpack."

"What are you guys even doing here?" I ask.

Sarah looks at me with what I can only describe as sympathy. "We want to find Zane. We thought if your podcast was true, we could help you break into the shipping containers to rescue them."

Oh.

Well, I guess that proves one thing—our podcast was believable if Dani and Sarah thought it was true. But how do I explain to them that it was all just a ruse to lure out Lizzie, who we think has answers that will lead us to Gloria, Seth, and Zane?

And after all the noise we've been making, and the light from the lantern, if Lizzie was in the woods—she's probably gone now. She could easily see it's six of us, not great odds for her.

"Well, it's not broken, and I think the bleeding has stopped. Just keep a little pressure on it," Max says to Dani, who is holding the rag to her face and pinching the bridge of her nose.

"Thanks Max," she says and glares at me.

Sarah lowers the lantern.

"Dani, really, I'm sorry. You just freaked me out, okay? I didn't mean to hurt you." I offer another, only kind of sincere, apology. I catch the way Nico's eyes crinkle in the light, and I know she's trying not to laugh. There will be plenty of time for that later, when we get out of the woods, because it really is kinda funny.

"Just shut up about it, okay? Now, are we going to go break our friends out of those shipping containers or what?" Dani says. She starts walking toward the big metal boxes, her combat boots padding softly across the dirt.

Sarah trots after her, her ponytail swinging side to side. I smile when I realize Dani and Sarah are both dressed in black like us. They really did come prepared to rescue their friend.

"Well, aren't you coming?" Dani asks when we don't immediately follow.

I let out a sigh. I look at my friends and shrug. "I mean, it doesn't hurt to check the containers, right? If Lizzie was here, she's probably gone now, with all the noise."

"Who's Lizzie?" Sarah asks as we catch up with them.

"No one," I say.

Now that we aren't trying to be stealthy, everyone has their phone lights on and the lantern is going. I feel silly with my boxing gloves dangling around my neck. Not really the weapons I thought they'd be, even though I did manage to get a punch in tonight.

Max lifts the metal bar and swings open the door on the first container. We hold our breath, waiting for someone to shine a light in, so we can see if our friends are inside. Even though I know they aren't, there's still a part of me wrapped up in this fake story, hoping it might be true. But the only things inside are pieces of wood and metal meant for the construction of the pavilion.

"Should we try the next one?" Nico asks. She takes a few steps toward the next rusted container. "Uh, guys, that's strange. There's a chain and lock on this one. But it looks brand new."

Everyone runs over to see, and sure enough, a bright, shiny silver chain and padlock are looped and locked around the metal arm that opens the back. Now why would someone lock this container and not the other?

"ZANE?" Dani pounds on the metal. "ZANE ARE YOU IN THERE?" she yells. Which causes all of us to yell, pound, and bang on the container. The noise is deafening in the night and all the crickets, night birds, and cicadas stop their evening song, startled by our sudden assault on the container. But in between the banging, I think I hear something.

"Wait! Stop and listen," I bark. Everyone stops and I put my ear to the metal. I close my eyes and listen. It's quiet at first, like an echo, but then I hear it louder.

Clang.

Clang.

Clang.

I jump back. "Did you hear that? Someone is in there!"

Sarah starts crying. "Zane, oh my God, she's in there."

Nico has her phone and is dialing 911.

Max slams his hand on metal and yells, "Gloria! I'm coming! Just hold on a little longer." He rushes back toward the equipment and grabs a piece of metal rebar. Then he shoves it in the links of the chain and starts to winch down on one side. "Grace, help me. We've got to try and break the chain."

But my knees feel weak... Gloria, Seth, and Zane might actually be in this shipping container. Locked in the dark, like animals in a cage. The air in my lungs constricts as my mind spins. Every sound is muffled and bleeds together—Nico telling the police where we are, Sarah still crying, Emma and Max grunting as they push on the metal, Dani muttering things to herself and pacing around in a confused state.

I realize I can do one of two things.

One: I can pass out from fear and PTSD—which is what my body is desperately trying to do... my legs are shaking and sweat is pouring from my brow. Pain radiates from behind my left eye as a migraine the size of Texas is forming.

Or two: I can suck it up, remind myself that I am strong, I am brave. I am not in a cage, I am free and I can rescue my friends.

I choose option two.

Chapter Twenty-Nine

BREAKING THE CHAINS

"The 911 lady says don't try to break the lock," Nico shouts. But there is no way in hell we can wait for first responders to show up with chain cutters! It'll take the police and fire trucks at least fifteen minutes to get all the way out here. That might not sound like a long time, but right now, it feels like infinity.

"Why not?" I demand.

Nico covers the phone and says, "She said we could get hurt. Or it could be a trap."

"Since when has that stopped us from doing anything before?" I ask. "Emma, here, let me try." I tap her on the shoulder and she steps out. Max's idea seems like it should work, using force to pop the chain apart. But the angle is wrong and the bar can't get enough leverage.

Max stops for a minute to catch his breath. He pushes his hair out of his eyes and looks closer at the chain and lock. "What if we stick the rebar into the lock and try popping it open that way? It looks pretty cheap," Max says. I step in and take a look. He's right. The chain is clearly new and heavy duty, but the lock, it's older—worn with some rust. It might break if we put enough force on it.

"Everyone back up. If we break the lock, it might go flying. Max, we should turn our heads away from it when we try this," I suggest. I really don't want to go blind from shards of metal shrapnel flying into my face.

"Back up," Nico orders Dani, Sarah, and Emma. They obey and take a few steps back. All of their lights are shining toward us now, illuminating the chain and lock.

"On the count of three," Max says.

I turn my head, close my eyes, tighten my grip—my muscles flex, aching to push down on the metal in my hands as hard as I can.

"One, two, THREE!"

I grunt and groan and don't feel any pain, just pressure in my hands as I put every ounce of my strength into breaking the lock. They say a mom can use superhuman strength to pick up a car if it's on top of her kid. That's what this feels like. Adrenaline courses through my body and I am no longer Grace Everly, teen with repressed memories of childhood trauma. I am Grace Everly, breaker of chains, rescuer of friends, finder of criminals...

POP!

Just as I was about to go further with my self-naming proclamation, the lock pops off. The sound is like a gunshot and everyone screams, including Max. Then more screams when we realize we can get inside the shipping container. Max pulls the chain, sliding it out of the metal arm latch, then he heaves the latch up and over. The door swings wide open.

Nico, Emma, Dani, and Sarah are right behind us with their phone lights.

And there, in the middle of the dusty shipping container, are Zane and Seth, gagged and bound to two average-looking wooden chairs.

"Holy shit," Max manages to say before we all pile in, screaming, crying, rejoicing to have found our friends.

Except this isn't everyone.

"Seth, thank God," I say between crying gulps. I pull the gag from his mouth and he sucks in air, while Nico and Emma work on untying his hands and feet from the chair. "Do you know where Gloria is?" I have to ask, before anything else, I need to know what happened to Gloria.

Now. Let's pause here. What are we doing wrong?

Anyone?

It's basically horror movie 101. Don't all go into one place at the same time. Especially when there is a bad guy or girl lurking about in the woods.

So it really shouldn't come as a surprise when the door to the container slams shut, plunging us all into darkness. The sound of the latch arm echoes inside the metal box. Which means it wasn't the wind blowing the heavy door shut, it was a person. A person who has just locked us inside.

But, hello!

We all have our cell phones. The container doesn't block signals. Plus, the police and first responders are already on their way. Of course, Dani and Sarah still scream and cry and bang on the door.

"HELP!"

"Let us out!"

"You won't get away with this!"

I think that's exactly what Lizzie is trying to do. Get away with this. Or at least get away from us right now. So, she hadn't been scared off by our banging. She was somewhere close, watching us, waiting to see if we'd find our friends.

Now, she's got at least a ten-minute head start to leave the woods before the first responders arrive, making it impossible for us to follow her.

"Stop all your shouting and finish untying Zane," I yell at Sarah and Dani. "Seth, are you hurt?" I want to ask him how long he's been in here, but a quick look around tells me not long. There's no sign of food or water.

"Grace," Seth exclaims as soon as his arms and feet are loose. He leaps out of the chair and wraps his arms around me. I bury my face into his chest and hold on to him. His body feels thin and he's trembling. "I knew you'd come. I told Gloria you'd find us," he says.

I step back and stare at my boyfriend. He's cuter than I remember, even if he's smelly and his face is kinda broken out and his hair is greasy. I'd give him a kiss, but he probably hasn't brushed his teeth in weeks. I can imagine his breath is kinda kidnap-victim funky.

"Seth, where is Gloria? We have to find her."

"She was with us. The woman brought us here in a van and made us carry these chairs out here. She had a gun and chains on our feet so we couldn't run. If we did, she'd be able to shoot us."

"But Gloria isn't here, it's just you and Zane," Max says.

"There was another container. Maybe she put Gloria in that one?" Nico suggests.

I shine the light further into the container, looking for clues. That's when I see a third chair, tipped over and lying on its side. I wonder if Gloria fought with the woman.

"Did Gloria escape?" I ask Seth.

He's busy chugging a bottle of water Max gave him.

I look over at Dani, Sarah, and Zane. Maybe Zane knows something. "Zane, I'm so glad we found you. We were all really worried."

Zane looks at me, her eyes wet from tears, and she says nothing. Instead, she just turns her head back and buries it in Dani's shoulder and keeps crying. Great. She's no help. So it's up to Seth to tell us what happened.

"You know, maybe Gloria did escape. Our mouths were gagged and we were blindfolded. The woman put me in the chair first, then Zane. I know because Zane is a loud crier, even with a gag." Seth glares at Zane. Now there's a topic we'll have to unpack later.

"Okay, so the woman marches you all out here, ties you and Zane up to the chairs, then maybe Gloria escapes when she is trying to tie her up. So she runs off to chase after Gloria, and that's when we arrive." It makes me feel more in control to say the timeline of events out loud.

"We didn't hear a gunshot in the woods," Max says.

"So, she didn't find Gloria, but she heard us. Probably when we were banging on the container," Nico says.

"Shouldn't the police be here by now?" Emma asks.

Nico looks at her phone. "Yeah, I called 911 like twenty minutes ago."

"Those assholes. They probably don't believe us. Well, maybe they'll believe this. Smile, Zane. Smile, Seth." I snap a couple of pictures of the recently found victims, post them on IG with the caption "Help! We are trapped in a shipping container at Fort McAllister #RescueMe #Victims" Then I tag the police department.

PING

BUZZ

DING

RING

That did it. Suddenly all our phones are blowing up. Everyone is on the phone with their parents and the sound inside the container is so loud. I give my phone to Seth so he can call his mom. I can hear her crying, no, sobbing on the other end. Seth turns his body away from us, and his shoulders start shaking. He's crying too. And I don't blame him one bit.

Max and I are the only ones not on our phones.

I look at him.

He looks at me.

"We have to find Gloria." I fold my arms over my chest.

I won't rest until I find that tall Dollface and tell her she's my best friend.

***

"Grace, you have to let the police do their job," Mom says. She's sitting next to me in the back seat. Dad's driving. It's 3 a.m. and we are finally going home. You should have seen it! They brought the SWAT team in to open the shipping containers. And they had police dogs and handlers searching the woods for Gloria and the kidnapper. Then, they brought in a helicopter with a spotlight! EMTs brought equipment on four wheelers with police who then took the four wheelers deeper out into the forest. It was a full-scale investigation.

Our parents showed up shortly after the SWAT team let us out of the container.

The problem was, it took forty minutes from our first 911 call for the cops to arrive. It wasn't until I posted the pictures that they took the call seriously. So, no matter how much they looked, they were never going to find Gloria or the woman.

I told the officer everything I could remember about Lizzie.

It had to be her.

There was no other person it could be.

I have this horrible nagging feeling that they really didn't take me seriously. They loaded up Zane and Seth to take them to the hospital for a full evaluation. Leaving me, Max, Nico, Emma, Sarah and Dani to be released to our parents.

The place was a total zoo.

And as much as I want to trust the police to find Gloria, I'm not sure I can. I'm kicking myself that I didn't ask Seth more about his captor. Was it really Lizzie? Did she use her name? Did I ask him her name?

Everything seems like a blur, as my adrenaline wanes.

"Dad, can you pull over at the Kwik Stop so I can get a Red Bull?" I ask.

"Grace Everly!" Mom gasps. "It's three in the morning."

"So what? I'm not going to sleep."

Dad grumbles something, then whips into the gas station parking lot, much to Mom's dismay. I get out of the car and run inside the brightly lit 24-hour convenience store. The lights are jarring after being in the dark forest for hours. I feel like I've stepped into a fantasy world filled with rainbow-colored rows of candy, cookies, and chips, all lined by coolers with every flavor soda imaginable. I grab two cans of Red Bull, some chips and cookies, and set them all on the counter. Dad gets himself a bottle of chocolate milk and plunks it down next to mine.

"Y'all know what's goin' on out there tonight? Seen least twenty cops and fire trucks and ambulances racing back and forth toward Fort McAllister all night," says the old woman behind the counter.

I shrug.

"Uh, nope," Dad says, tapping his card on the Apple Pay.

I grab my stuff and turn around, ready to get home and call my friends to figure out our next move. But the woman's not done talking.

"Rats. I love a good police chase story. Woman came in earlier, thought maybe she the one who called 'em, but she just shook her head."

My feet freeze to the polished linoleum floor.

"Come on, Grace, Mom is waiting." Dad puts his hand on my shoulder as he breezes by me. I don't move.

"What was that?" I mumble.

"Huh sweetie? You talkin' to me?" the woman asks.

I will my feet to unfreeze so I can turn around to look at her. "Why did you think the woman was the one who called the police?"

"Cause she was laughin' when she walked in. I asked her what was so funny and she said them cops ain't gonna find what they lookin' for."

"That's a weird thing to say," I reply. Oh my God, could the woman be Lizzie?

"That's what I thought. So I asked if she was the one who called the cops. She just shook her head, bought some duct tape and water and left."

It has to be her. I'm about to open my mouth to say so, but Dad's behind me, with his phone out. "Can you tell the police exactly what you just told my daughter? That sounds like the woman they are looking for. Do your cameras work yet?"

"Sure thing. And yeah, after that little girl got snatched from the high school, corporate came 'round from Atlanta and fixed our CCTV. Got it right in the back." The woman's eyes light up. She grins, showing off a couple of missing teeth. I can see the wheels turning in her head as she realizes her shift is about to get a lot more exciting.

"Can you show me the video before the police come?" I ask. "I have to see her, I'll recognize her."

But Dad puts his free arm out to stop me from walking with the woman to the back office. "Grace, we should wait for the police—" He stops speaking to me and starts talking on his phone when 911 answers. "Yes, hello, this is Mr. Everly, I'm at the Kwik Stop and..."

I duck under his arm and look at the woman. Her name badge says *Patricia*.

"Patricia, please, can you show it to me? I think that woman kidnapped my friend Gloria. I need to see her face," I beg.

Dad is pacing around the store trying to convince the emergency operator that this is in fact an emergency and an officer should come out and take a witness statement from Patricia. It's now or never. I look Patricia in the eyes, willing mine to water, and let my bottom lip quiver.

"Please. You'll be a hero."

Bingo.

"You think I'll get to speak on the news?" Patricia asks, her voice aching for recognition.

"Yes ma'am!" I exclaim. "Hurry, the cops will be here soon and you wanna make sure you see the video so you can nail the interview."

A sly smile spreads over her face. "Girl, you right. I don't wanna say it happened one way, but really it happened another."

I nod and follow Patricia into the back office where she plunks down in a chair at a computer screen. The new CCTV equipment is shiny and there's an instruction sheet pinned up on the wall, explaining how to watch the recordings. Very helpful, since after a few tries, Patricia shrugs. She looks over her shoulder and says, "I dunno, you wanna give it a try?"

"Yes, I think we just have to press—" I lean over her and tap the F3 key and the recording from the last 24 hours pops up on the screen.

"Hey, how'd you do that?" She shakes her head. "You kids, always on them phones, know how to do it all these days."

I just ignore her jab at my age and tech skills, reaching over her again and pushing the forward arrow to get to the right digital frame. She said the woman came in shortly after the police cars were heading toward Fort McAllister. The police didn't arrive for forty minutes after Nico first called. Which means Lizzie had enough time to get back to her vehicle, lock Gloria inside, drive out of the woods and make it here.

Which means, if I'm right, I should see the mystery woman around midnight.

The screen flicks forward, frame at a time, until— "There! That's her!" I shout.

Patricia and I lean in, watching as a woman in jeans and a sweatshirt walks into the mart, sauntering over to the counter. Her hair is dark and she has on sunglasses. Like that's not suspicious at night. She glances hastily over her shoulder a few times, but I can't get a good view of her face from that angle. But something doesn't feel right... in my memories, Lizzie had blonde hair. Not that that means a thing. Girls dye their hair all the time.

"Are there other angles? So I can see her face?" I ask.

"Now that I *do* know how to do. Just gotta push this key for the view behind the counter." She pushes F8 and the view changes. Giving me a perfect view of the woman.

I was expecting it to be Lizzie.

I stumble back, slamming into the wall of the tiny office when I see the face. I'd recognize it anywhere, even with sunglasses on.

"No way." I'm in shock.

Standing at the Kwik Stop counter isn't Lizzie, or even my therapist Tammy, because if we're being real here, she's been acting pretty sketchy.

No.

The person standing at the counter is Gloria's mom, Daisy Sanchez.

"DAAAaaaddd!" I scream. He has to see this. He has to know I'm telling the truth.

"Grace, are you okay?" he bellows and comes charging into the back room.

I point at the screen. Patricia slides over, giving Dad a better view. Her grin is massive and she's shaking her head. "Damn this is exciting. Who is it?" She looks at me, then at Dad.

"No. That can't be right. We don't know why she was here, Grace. No. She can't be involved." He's rubbing his face and shaking his head.

With trembling hands, I pull my phone out and take a picture of the screen.

"Is there video from the parking lot? Can we see what vehicle she was driving?" I ask. Dad is on his phone calling someone. Maybe the police, maybe Mom, I don't know, but he steps aside as Patricia taps another button, switching the camera view to an image of the parking lot. We watch as Gloria's mom walks out of the store with duct tape and bottled water and gets into a dark van. Just like the one that kidnapped Gloria. Just like the kind Mr. Sanchez uses at his tile installation company. I've seen the various vans parked at their house plenty of times.

That's proof enough for me.

I walk out of the small room and into the bright lights of the convenience store, feeling less and less like I want the Red Bull in my hand and more and more like I want a big can of justice for Gloria.

How the hell could her own mom kidnap her?

There's only one way to find out.

Chapter Thirty

THE KEY

I'm living next door to a kidnapper. No. Scratch that. I'm living next door to a psychopath. But it's not Gloria—like I once accused her of being. Okay, so maybe I accused her of being a psychopath all the time. Can you fault me? Do I have to remind you that she never talks to me, which has really messed with my head all these years? But anyway...

The real psychopath is her mom, the picture-perfect *Daisy Sanchez.*

I rap my knuckles on my head. Why didn't I think of it sooner?

"Gah! I feel so stupid," I say to Mr. Puppy. I'm sitting on my bed with his floppy face in my lap. My parents are downstairs at the table, drinking coffee and trying to sort through this mess. As soon as the police arrived at the Kwik Stop to interview Patricia, we left to come home. I have no idea if they are going to take the lead seriously or not. But I know it's her. I can feel it in my bones. Which means our Lizzie lead was just a ruse.

"Does Lizzie really exist, Mr. Puppy?" Or—as my parents told me as a child—she was just in my dreams. A coping mechanism. I'm not sure I can trust any of my memories anymore. Not until I sit down and have a frank conversation with Tammy.

"Yeah, she does exist, remember, we saw her name in your file," Nico says.

"AGH!" I scream and turn around. Nico, Emma, and Max are standing in my doorway. I leap off my bed and throw my arms around my friends. "What are you guys doing here? I thought you were all asleep by now!"

"We got your text, about Gloria's mom. Do you think we were just gonna let you sit here and deal with that alone?" Emma asks.

"But your parents?" I ask.

"Snuck out," Max says.

"Cried," Nico says.

"My mom is downstairs. She drove us." Emma smiles.

"Wait, Nico, you cried?" I'm mildly shocked.

"You remember I tried out for the school play last year. And Mrs. Allen said I lacked emotion." Nico's lower lip trembles and she bats her dark eyelashes a few times before a sly smile spreads over her face. "Bullshit. See, I'm full of emotion, well at least enough to convince my parents to release me to Emma's mom when they came to pick me up."

"Brilliant! You guys are the best." And I mean it. They really are the best.

"So, what do we do now?" Max asks.

Hmmm... that is the question, isn't it? What do we do now? I wish we could talk to Seth and Zane, to hear their side of the story. But I've tried calling Seth and texting him. It's still going to voicemail. Which means he must still be at the hospital. Because, if he was home, he'd be calling me.

I wonder if Zane is reachable.

Would she answer my questions if I called her?

"Grace, what's happening? You're making a weird face. Don't break your brain." Nico goes over and flops on my bed and pats the spot next to her.

"Seth isn't answering his phone. We could try reaching Zane," I suggest.

"If you're sure that was Mrs. Sanchez, then why don't we just go next door and break in? Do they have a basement? Maybe she brought Gloria home and locked her in the basement." Max clenches his jaw.

"Or maybe they went on the lam," Emma exclaims. "Maybe Mr. Sanchez was in on it too and the house will be empty, and it will be like Gloria never existed at all. You know, like they'll disappear to Mexico or Canada."

"Really, Emma?" Nico rolls her eyes.

"You know, she's not wrong. That would be the smartest thing to do, go on the run. Why risk being caught here in town?" I pull my knees up to my chest and rest my chin on them. The sky is starting to lighten outside. I can't believe everything that's happened in the last twenty-four hours.

"Y'all, if we sit around here much longer, I'm gonna fall asleep," Nico says with a yawn.

Maybe we all should pile on my bed and do just that.

Let the cops track down Daisy and find Gloria.

But... what if...well, what if something really bad happens to Gloria? If her mom was willing to do all those kidnappings and lie right to our faces, what else is she capable of? Murder? Because you don't buy duct tape in the middle of the night unless you're planning on wrapping a body up to dump it somewhere.

"Let's go see if Mr. Sanchez is home," I announce.

Me and my friends pile out of my room and run down the stairs like a herd of wildebeests. I peek in the kitchen where Emma's mom is sitting with my parents at the table; they are deep in conversation.

"Just have to grab something outside, be back in a flash," I shout into the kitchen as my friends exit through the front door.

"Grace, wait, no—we don't want you kids getting any more involved, not now," Dad says and stands up. But I'm already halfway out the door. I close it tightly behind me and yell, "Run!"

Nico, Emma, and Max dart off the porch and run through the grass over to Gloria's house. It's dark, quiet, and empty. No lights on. No signs of life at all. I ring the doorbell. Once, twice, three times, then I start ringing it DING-DONG-DING-DONG. Since when did they have a Ring Cam?

I put my ear up to the door and listen. Then I rattle it and try to open it.

"Grace, I don't think anyone is home," Max says.

"Like that's gonna stop her." Nico laughs.

I remember the silver spare key, I've seen Gloria use it before, hidden under the farthest planter on the porch. That Dollface better have remembered to put it back before she was kidnapped, because I really need to break into her house and check every room and closet to make sure she wasn't tied up and left to rot.

If I thought she was screwed up before all this, I can only imagine the therapy bill she's gonna have as an adult.

To know it was her own mom, all along. You think you know someone, like really know them, and then they turn out to be just another monster lurking in the woods. I'd say it's a tragedy, but that's just pointing out the obvious.

I return to the door with the key, sliding it into the lock.

"And just what do you think you're doing?" Dad asks. We all scream and jump a foot in the humid early morning air.

"God, Dad! Don't sneak up on people when they are breaking into a house," I scold him.

"I don't think Rafael would appreciate you kids going in there," Dad says.

"You know that was Daisy on the video feed at the Kwik Stop! They aren't answering the door. We have to find out what happened to Gloria, please Dad. Come inside with us. Let's just see if there are any clues," I beg him. "If Mr. Sanchez isn't answering the door right now, maybe he's in on it too."

Dad lets out a long sigh. "Your mom is gonna kill me." Then he coughs once, and says, "I don't mean that. She would never actually hurt me."

I roll my eyes and Emma and Nico laugh. Dad opens the door, going inside first. It's dark and he turns on the entryway light. "Hello, neighbors, anyone home?"

We creep in behind Dad, all four of us using him as a human shield in case any weird shit happens. Like Mrs. Sanchez comes running out with a butcher knife or something. But the house is quiet. No one says anything and Dad takes a few more steps forward into the living room. He flicks on the light. "All clear," he says. "Well, I guess they aren't home. If you kids want to do a quick run through the house and check the rooms, just to be safe. But no lingering," he lectures us.

We don't have to be told twice.

Max runs for the kitchen. Emma rushes for the back. Nico and I take the stairs two at a time to get to the second floor as fast as we can. We split up, dashing in and out of the bedrooms, checking in the closets and behind the curtains.

No sign of Gloria.

There's only one room left to check.

Gloria's.

Chapter Thirty-One

CAN YOU HANDLE THE TRUTH?

My hand is trembling. I've been here twice without Gloria, and the entire time all I wanted deep down in my gut was for that big dummy to be sitting on her bed and to jump up and throw her arms around me in a bear hug. I don't even care if she doesn't talk to me. I just want to know she's safe and alive. But now there's this tension in my body, a fear that I can't explain. I'm terrified that when I open the door, Gloria is going to be dead. Her flesh twisted on the floor in a big, bloody heap.

"Well go on," Nico urges.

I suck in my breath, turn the knob, and push the door open.

"Hi Grace, I wondered if you'd come rescue me." Gloria is in the center of her room, duct-taped to her desk chair. Her usually clean dark hair is dirty and disheveled. She looks tired and beaten. Not physically—but emotionally. Her eyes are sunk in and her cheeks stained with tear streaks.

I'm frozen.

Staring at the girl who hasn't spoken to me since we were children.

Why didn't she cry out for help when she heard us coming?

Why can't I move to go untie her?

Nico shoves me to get by. "Holy shit, Gloria! It's really you. You're alive." Nico falls to her knees and starts tearing at the duct tape. "GUYS! SHE'S HERE!" Nico screams for Max, Emma and my dad.

There are a million things running through my mind, pinging off every nerve. A million questions I have for Gloria. But when I move my lips to make words, they don't form. Nothing I want to say sounds right. Like how fucked-up would it be for me to ask her, *Why did your mom kidnap you?* As if I have any right to ask that. Maybe I should ask her if she's thirsty or hungry. I mean, she looks thin. Like she hasn't had anything in weeks. Her lips are cracked and peeling, her cheeks ghostly hollow.

"Thanks Nico, God, my mom is such a whack job. I can't believe she did this to me," Gloria says. Her voice—it sounds like it does when I catch her talking at school. But it's still foreign to me. My ears don't register it as Gloria's voice. The voice in my head the last few weeks has been of her as a kid, all my memories of us locked in the rotten-faced man's dog cages.

Dad, Max, and Emma rush into the room, and my limp body is easily shoved aside. I press my back against the wall, using it to keep me standing upright. Watching as Dad and Max finish ripping the tape off Gloria's wrists that were secured behind her back. I guess now we know why Daisy was buying the duct tape.

"Gloria, oh my God, sweetheart, are you hurt, is anything broken?" Dad asks. "Max, call the police. We need an ambulance."

Gloria stands up and stretches. "I'm fine. Thanks for breaking me free."

I'm watching her with fascination.

No, I'm studying her. Each movement, each reaction, not what I imagined her to be like. She's different, more sure of herself. Or maybe I'm just less sure of myself. Why haven't I said anything yet? Or smiled?

This was what I've been utterly obsessed with for the last few weeks, finding Gloria. So why am I not more happy? Why does my face feel like this? Heavy, sad.

"Why don't we all go downstairs and wait for the police. I'm sure they are going to have a ton of questions for you, Gloria," Dad says. He leads the way, and Max puts his arm around Gloria to help guide her, I suppose in case she really isn't as 'fine' as she claims. Emma and Nico follow close behind, but I can't move.

"Come on Grace, aren't you coming?" Emma pauses and reaches a handout to me.

I look down at my hand and turn it over a few times, examining it. It works, but it doesn't stretch out to grab Emma's.

"Emma, Grace, you coming?" Nico yells from the hallway.

"We should go downstairs," Emma says.

There's noise and commotion coming from downstairs. Mom and Emma's mom—Dad must have called our house. I can't make out what they are saying, but I can tell it's them from their loud clucking. Probably shocked to see emaciated Gloria and going into full mom mode to clean, wash, feed, and wrap her in blankets. The sound of sirens in the distance grow closer and closer.

Emma is bouncing from foot to foot, clearly torn about wanting to stay with me or go downstairs to be where all the action is. I don't blame her. I want to be where the action is too! I want to know what happened to Gloria and where her parents have gone. But I can't get myself to move. Finally, when the sirens are nearly at the house, Emma forcefully grabs my arm and drags me with her.

"You must be in shock," she says, as she guides me out of Gloria's room and down the stairs.

I nod, or at least, I think I do.

Emma tugs me into the living room and plunks me down on the couch, pulls a crocheted blanket off the back and wraps it around me. Then she wanders off toward the kitchen, where everyone else has congregated. I don't have a great view, but I can hear things.

Things I don't want to hear.

The police have arrived.

They ask tough questions.

Gloria cries.

Mom and Dad console her.

Revelations spew from Gloria's mouth about the kind of woman Daisy Sanchez really was behind closed doors. Mean. Angry. Bitter. She blamed Gloria for the 'breakup' with my parents. Because she wouldn't talk to me.

"For a long time, I didn't know I wasn't talking to her," Gloria sobs. "Grace was always so happy, she didn't seem to remember what happened to us, so I never had anything to say."

The police don't care.

They want to know where Daisy and Rafael are.

"Dad didn't have anything to do with it!" Gloria screams. "It was all her. She did this. She locked us in the back room of the warehouse."

"Okay, Gloria, calm down. Where is your dad right now—if he isn't part of this, where is he?" an officer asks her.

I roll my eyes. Duh, idiot. Obviously, Daisy has him gagged and bound somewhere. Unless she killed him. Oh God, what if she killed him? That would be seriously fucked-up. I'm having a hard time picturing Daisy as the mastermind of this whole thing, let alone as someone capable of killing her husband. But—that smile, that laugh, that bounce in her step when she was on camera at the Kwik Stop flashes through my mind.

That woman. She could kill her husband.

The sunlight dances on the wall in front of me, streaming in through the front windows. Gloria says something, answers a question I didn't hear. But the more I strain my ears to hear, the more I hear nothing at all. I sink back into the couch, feeling my energy, or what is left of it, wane. I never drank the Red Bull and I'm crashing. My head leans, my body follows, and before I know it, I'm lying down with my eyes closed.

I don't remember Dad carrying me home.

I don't remember if I have any dreams.

When I wake up, it's dark outside and I'm drowning in my sheets and blankets. My heartbeat quickens in my chest, and I swim with all my might, fighting against the currents, just hoping to hold my head above water. I gasp for air and sit up in my bed.

"And she wakes," a familiar voice. "But does she speak?"

"Seth!" I exclaim.

My boyfriend climbs onto my bed and throws his arms around me. He is a lifeboat in this sea of uneasiness.

"Don't worry, I haven't been here for long. But your mom said I could come up, that you'd been sleeping all day," he says. His words are kind of mumbly and his breath is hot on my neck. His face is buried into my hair, and he squeezes me hard, like he's afraid I might disappear if he lets go.

"I don't care about that! Watch me as long as you like. I'm so glad you're here and you're okay. I've been so worried." My voice is shaky. I'm not sure I can stop myself from crying. But I want to be strong for him.

"Man, it was so fucked up. I mean, I've never been more bored in my entire life." He finally lets go of me and we sit apart and I get a chance to really look at him.

"Wait, what?" I shake my head. "You were bored? Like, you'd been kidnapped, were being held hostage, and you were bored?"

"Yeah, I mean, we were locked in some little office room all day with nothing to do. If I had to listen to Zane and Gloria a second longer, I was going to stick my head in the toilet. And that thing was fucking gross, so—"

I can't tell if he's being serious or not.

"Wait, so Gloria's mom kidnaps you three and just leaves you locked in a room for two weeks and that's it? What the fuck was her problem?"

"She never talked to me or Zane. Just Gloria, and damn was she mean to her. Every time she brought us food, she'd really lay into Gloria. Kept threatening to lock her in a dog cage. Said that was the only way to break her." Seth shakes his head. "After a while, Gloria told Zane about what happened to you two, you know, when you were kids."

He looks at me with big sad eyes.

"Well, I didn't remember any of it until Gloria was taken. So don't look at me like that—okay." I give him a little shove. I can't stand him looking at me like he feels sorry for me when he's the one who's been held hostage for weeks. What happened to me was a long time ago and I'm not that scared little girl anymore. I'm not even the same scared girl I was yesterday. Today, I have everything back. I have Seth. Zane is alive. Which, let's all be honest, is kind of a bummer, because she's still a bitch. And Gloria. She speaks.

I let out a long sigh.

"Yeah, I'll try..." He pauses, then scratches his head and shakes his black hair from his eyes and sniffs the air. "Smells like your mom made dinner. You wanna go downstairs and get something to eat?"

"You mean, she put something in the oven she bought from Cost-co. I didn't think you liked eating here."

"I don't care what it is, only eating a PB&J and banana every day for two weeks has me rethinking food," he says.

"Oh yeah?" My eyebrows raise. Seth's a notoriously picky eater.

"That was probably the worst part, feeling hungry all the time. Mom said she's gonna feed me six meals a day for the rest of my life." He laughs, but it's strained, and there's sadness behind it. Maybe even fear. Something clatters in the kitchen downstairs and he practically jumps a foot.

"Food. Yes, whatever you want, that sounds great." I lean in and give Seth a kiss. My lips rejoice against his, even if they are still kind of chapped from being dehydrated for weeks. I crawl off my bed, link hands with Seth, and together we leave my bedroom and head out to face the world. I know he's trying to act like it was so boring being locked in that room for two weeks, that he didn't care, but deep down I'm sure he's grappling with a lot of heavy emotions.

"Maybe after dinner we can go back to your house so you can play *Warzone* with your friends and I'll watch," I suggest.

He nods. "Yeah, those assholes have been texting me all day. They leveled up while I was gone... really, you don't mind me playing?"

"I just want to get back to normal."

"Me too," he says and leans over to kiss me one more time before we walk into the kitchen.

Mom's dishing up homemade spaghetti and meatballs while Dad is mixing up a huge bowl of Caesar salad.

"My favorite!" Seth rushes to help my mom carry the food to the table. He's got a bite in his mouth before anyone else is even sitting down. "Mmmm, Mrs. Everly, you're such a good cook," he says with a mouthful of noodles and sauce.

Dad looks at me, then at Mom, and we all three burst out laughing. Seth is oblivious as he shovels the food in faster than seems humanly possible. I open my mouth to tell him to slow down, but Mom catches my eyes and shakes her head.

"I'm sure you're famished, Seth. Here, let me put more on your plate."

"We're glad to have you back, Seth." Dad's voice cracks.

"Mmmme too." Seth nods, his fork diving to spear another meatball to shove into his already full mouth.

He really wasn't kidding when he said he'd been starving for two weeks. My knee-jerk reaction is anger. But what good would that do, if I started yelling and cursing about Mrs. Sanchez and what she did. The best thing for Seth is to be there for him, like I know he's going to be there for me. I load my plate up with garlic bread and salad and listen as Dad tells us a story from his gym and Mom talks about some cooking classes she'd like to take.

Chapter Thirty-Two

Hellhounds (Two Months Later)

There's still a lot of shit I have to work through, like why I clam up like a shellfish protecting a pearl every time I'm around Gloria. Oh, what, you don't believe me? Look what happened to us yesterday morning…

"GRACE!" she bellowed outside the front door.

I was still in the kitchen, grabbing a string cheese to eat on the way to school. Mom, in that ugly floral apron, smiled at me. "Have a great day."

"Oh, don't forget, I'm going to Max's house after boxing practice to record the next episode of the podcast. I'll be home by ten." Then I ran out the front door, happy, healthy, and normal. But as soon as I saw Gloria, my heart clenched inside my chest—like it was tied up with a rope, or duct tape. My smile faded, and my voice disappeared.

Don't get me wrong!

I'm always so happy to see her. I even jumped off the porch and ran up to give her a big hug.

"Still?" she asked when I didn't say anything.

I nodded silently.

"Don't worry, I have plenty to tell you," and she did. Oh, did she ever! Gloria told me all about the major drama in her third period class between Sarah and Benji. It was so juicy! She chatted at me the entire way to school, and I listened, sifting through every bit of gossip in my head. She really is an incredible storyteller. It sucks it's taken her this long to feel comfortable around me, and it sucks even more that I've become the mute one. I can't even ask any follow-up questions! Like, *wait, what did he say*? Or *oh no way, she didn't do that*! Or anything else. But Gloria usually does a pretty good job regardless.

So yep. See what I mean?

Now, I'm the freak show.

In case you were wondering, the cops found her dad Rafael tied up in a ditch on the side of the highway near Valdosta, with no signs of Daisy. He was just as dumbfounded as Gloria—why Daisy snapped one day and started kidnapping kids. But at least he's alive and Gloria didn't lose both her parents. It's hard to tell if they are happy Daisy is gone—or sad. That's one subject Gloria avoids like the plague on our walks to school. She never, ever speaks about her mom or what happened leading up to the kidnappings.

Mom is worried Daisy might come back and try something again.

But the cops don't think so.

They traced her to Texas before they lost track of her... or before she figured out they were tracking her and she ditched her credit cards and traded cars. Who knows.

But one thing I do know is this...

Things in our town might not be as mysterious as Hawkins, Indiana. But there's definitely things lurking in the woods. Ghosts, rotten-faced men, angry, bitter women, asshole therapists brainwashing kids (don't even get me started on Tammy).

***

ME: *Hey all you freaks and geeks. Welcome back to another episode of—*

NICO, EMMA & ME (All together): *What's in the Woods?*

Max smiles and plays a new music intro sequence he's been working on. It's a total jam and we all throw our hands up in the air and dance in our seats for a few seconds before he nods to start the show.

EMMA: *Max! That intro was a banger!*

NICO, EMMA & ME (All together, clapping): *Ahhhoooooo!*

MAX (laughing): *Thanks guys. I'm getting more serious about producing my own music. Now that Gloria's back, she's been helping me write most of the melodies.*

NICO (leans into her microphone): *Ooooh, Max and Gloria sitting in a tree, K-I-S-S-I-N-G.*

MAX (blushing): *Umm... yeah, we do like to kiss. Sorry babe, they called me out.*

NICO, EMMA & ME (All whistling and making kissy face sounds)

ME: *Okay, okay, now that we're caught up on Max and Gloria's love life, let's dig into the next mystery. This is one my own boyfriend Seth heard a few weeks ago. It's about a pack of wild dogs that live out on the mudflats.*

NICO: *What's so scary about that?*

ME: *Well, this isn't just any pack of wild dogs, this is a pack of Hellhounds!*

For the next thirty minutes, me and my friends spin wild tales about sightings of Hellhounds around town. We laugh, joke around, and have a blast. I love that Max is now a permanent part of our podcast crew and he let us keep our studio in his backyard shed. I also love that he's dating Gloria. They really are super cute together.

So yeah, I guess that's my story.

There's still a lot of unanswered questions about what happened to me and Gloria during our time with the rotten-faced man. And one of these days, I'll get my voice back and we'll be able to talk about it. Or maybe not. Maybe those horrors are better left buried, and after everything else that happened to her, Gloria might never want to relieve that trauma.

My migraines have stopped completely and I don't have to take any meds. So I'm calling that a big win. I think all the memories inside of me just wanted so badly to get out that they were willing to nearly incapacitate me with pain in the process.

And another pain point that's been solved: Mom said Lizzie Kemper reached out to her last week!

She admitted to sending us that email—the one that told us about her older brother dying in the car accident. Sounds like she actually is a librarian now, for some small town in the mountains outside of Atlanta. She was never here, in Richmond Hill. She just happened to stumble upon our podcast when she was snooping around following up on me and Gloria. She wanted to apologize for not coming forward sooner and for lying to get a job as an intern with Tammy, but she said she was young and stupid and panicked.

I told Mom that was a bunch of bullshit.

She told me to watch my language.

And we haven't talked about it since.

There is one last question that keeps me up at night... and I dunno if it even matters anymore. Because without it, Gloria, Seth, and Zane might all be dead, my memories would still be locked away inside my head, and I wouldn't be boxing at Dad's gym three nights a week. Plus,

I wouldn't be looking at colleges for film and media production. Yeah, I'm going to try and do this podcast thing full time, maybe even get into scriptwriting.

The thing that weighs on me, those two little words, scrawled in neat handwriting on a scrap of inconspicuous paper...

One day I'll ask Gloria what she meant when she wrote: *Ask Grace*.

But today is not that day.

Acknowledgements

First, I have to thank my loving husband and children for supporting me during my long nights, early mornings, and pretty much every single, silly weekend. I know I spend a lot of time writing, revising, and editing. It is both my art and my addiction. But never forget that you are always my reason... I intend on providing the life that you all want and deserve, now and forever. Because, heck, you've earned it!

To my Daddy, I love you more than all the stars, because they go on forever and ever.

To Abigail Wild, founder of Wild Ink Publishing, and the hardest working woman I know. You are a rock star human being. It is a pleasure to work with you and I can never thank you enough for believing in my words and continuing to publish my stories. I love you.

To Andie Smith, my kind-hearted and intelligent editor. Thank you so much for your availability, support, and encouragement during the revision process. And not judging me for my ridiculous use of commas.

To Dana Hawkins, you know what you did last summer. (HA! Actually, I have no idea, I just know we are on fire and I love you more than words. Current mission if you choose to accept: a VW Bus to travel and write across the lands in—we may or may not come out alive).

I have many friends in the writing world, but there are a few very near and dear to my heart I would like to thank: Ginny Myers Sain, Casie Bazay, Jenni Howell, Alyssa Villaire, Tracy Truels, Vanessa Montalban, Theresa Green, E.L. Johnson, Emily St. Marie, Abigail F. Taylor, Demi Michelle Schwartz, Diane Billas, Mariah Stillbrook, Bruce Buchanan, Amy Nielsen, and Benjamin Cloth.

Thank you to my loving family scattered all over the world as well as my kind and supportive friends at BRPSC.

About the S.E. Reed

S.E. has spent the last 20 years of her life moving around all five-regions of the United States which gives her a unique American perspective. Many of her pieces have a strong Southern theme, but she also dabbles in the strange, bizarre and fantastical.

Her work has been featured by Wild Ink Publishing, Parhelion Lit, The Writer's Workout, Tempered Rune's Press and Survival Guide for the 21st Century. She has won several YA writing contests and actively participates as a delegate for YA Hub on Twitter.

S.E. resides in Florida with her family– nestled between the swamps of the Everglades and the salt of the Atlantic Ocean. This summer she'll be sitting in a lawn chair, working on her next novel and listening to EDM... (Ask her about her days as a DJ). Or she'll be in the pool begging her kids not to get her hair wet.

You can find S.E. Reed in the following places:

www.writingwithreed.com